THE DO

Rose McDonagh was born in Edinburgh. Her writing has won the Bath Flash Fiction Award and been shortlisted for the Bridport Prize, the London Magazine Short Story Competition, the Dinesh Allirajah Prize and the Bristol Prize. She was longlisted for the Caledonia First Novel Award and the Lucy Cavendish Fiction Prize. She is trained as a counsellor and has many years' experience working in community health. She lives in Scotland with her husband and two cats.

The Dog Husband

Rose McDonagh

REFLEX PRESS

First published as a collection in 2022 by Reflex Press
Abingdon, Oxfordshire, OX14 3SY
www.reflex.press

A CIP catalogue record of this book is
available from the British Library.

ISBN: 978-1-914114-06-9

1 3 5 7 9 10 8 6 4 2

Printed and bound in Great Britain by
Severn, Gloucester.

Cover image by Freddie Marriage

www.reflex.press/the-dog-husband/

To mum, dad, and my brother Steven.
With love always.

CONTENTS

The Mute Swan

'Like a clown?'

'Come on. Mute, not a mime.'

'As in deaf-mute?'

'No, just not speaking. She can hear. You're acting like it's funny.'

'I'm not,' I said. 'I just want to understand. So it's a physical thing? She can't physically speak?'

'No. He didn't say that. I'm pretty sure it's psychological. Listen, he thought you'd make a joke out of it. That's why he asked me to tell you first.'

'Me? You're worse than I am.'

'We're both pretty bad. Let's catch up and get all the jokes out the way, and then we can meet her without saying anything too awful.'

Our friend Christopher had a new girlfriend. We had rarely liked anyone he chose to date. When Tess told me about this one, I was hopeful. The speech problem made me think she might be less judgemental than the others. Tess and I met at the café on the corner nearest our two flats, sliding into our regular booth by the window. Tess had dyed her hair with streaks of cobalt since I'd seen her the week before. We did make a few jokes about this new person, but we only really wanted her to be kind. We ordered waffles and coffee. Beside us, the giant windowpane was hazed with condensation so that the people outside seemed to battle through fog. We talked until the staff began to mop the chequered floor.

The girlfriend's name was Ella. I met her two weeks later when there was a last-minute plan to spend a weekend in a cottage up near Inverness. It was early March, and someone from the bar where Christopher worked had been unexpectedly unable to use the place.

On a drizzling Friday evening, I squashed into the back of Christopher's car, lumping my rucksack onto my knees. Ella was sitting up front. I could see a strip of her face in the passenger visor mirror. She had neat, dark eyes, a long nose, wide, natural eyebrows. Tess was already sitting in the other back seat, her suitcase wedged between us. The car had a faint smell that I couldn't put my finger on, except it reminded me of something from childhood.

'Nice to meet you, Ella,' I said.

I glanced to see if she nodded, but she didn't seem to respond at all. 'Hope everyone brought waterproofs and booze,' Christopher said.

The journey was long, and Ella was, of course, silent, but Christopher spoke to her, making comments on the scenery or things he'd remembered or forgotten to pack, and her head did occasionally bob in response.

When we stopped at a service station, Christopher got out, and Ella slid from her seat and followed him. She was wearing jeans and a heavy woollen jumper. She was short, and slightly chubby, different in appearance from his other girlfriends. Despite my intention to be tolerant, I found it eerie the way she trailed after him without a word, as if she was his shadow unstitched.

'Well, what do you think of our mute swan?' Tess turned to me, grinning.

'I don't know yet. She might be nice.'

'She might be. She doesn't exactly seem warm.'

'It's hard to come across as warm if you don't talk. Does she smile? I can't see from here.'

'Yeah,' Tess said. 'She has smiled sometimes. When he put the heater on, and when we stopped.'

They returned to the car, Christopher carrying a bottle of coke, Ella clutching a packet of crisps and a large caramel bar. I have always liked a person with an unfussy appetite, so this endeared her to me a little. We drove on, Tess taking a turn at the wheel, Christopher sitting in the back with me.

The sky darkened, the trees by the roadside transformed into grasping figures. Bottles clinked in the boot as we followed a lolling single-track road. We arrived in complete darkness, pulling into a gravel drive. The cottage sat on the edge of a sea-loch with a few others dotted either side. I couldn't make out much else of the surroundings. Inside, the place was sparsely furnished, the stone walls left bare and rough, a real fireplace in the living room. The building had been made by adding an extension to a much older core.

We discovered firelighters in a drawer in the kitchen, old newspapers and kindling left out in a basket. In time, we got a blaze going and fed in a few large, dry hunks of wood. We settled in front of the television to watch a German film Tess had brought. Christopher and Ella took their place on the couch, Tess and me sank into an armchair each. The film was confusing, it had a modern setting, but the plot seemed to mash together different fairy tales, and all of it in black and white despite being recently made. Soon, Ella fell asleep on Christopher's shoulder. She looked small and vulnerable and

I found myself feeling almost protective of her. Outside, the wind was up, searching round the corners of the cottage. I must have dozed too because I woke to Tess saying, 'Bloody hell, it's a good film. Yous are not even trying.'

'Sorry, I'm knackered,' I said.

Ella rubbed her eyes and looked round the room.

'I think we're calling it a night,' Christopher said, squeezing her against his side.

He and Ella retired to a double room at the end of the corridor. Tess and I were to share a twin room opposite the shower. 'We're the kids in this family,' Tess said as we dug our pyjamas out of our bags, pulled the tightly tucked sheets from under the mattresses. I couldn't help wondering if we would overhear anything from Christopher and Ella's room, if she would make any kind of sound in the night. A snore or squeak or gasp. All was quiet as I stretched my legs under the sheets. I was tired from the day at work. Sleep rapidly pulled me under so that I heard nothing.

When the morning came, and I padded through to the kitchen, Ella was sitting at the breakfast table in her T-shirt and pyjama bottoms, eating oat flakes from a bowl. She smiled. In the sunlight, she looked ordinary and kind. I sat opposite in peaceable silence, eating a fruit yogurt as we waited for the others to join us.

The four of us headed out for a walk. The landscape had the dowdy, respectable colours of a female pheasant. Spring hadn't reached this far north yet.

When we came to a more remote part of the loch, Christopher turned to face the water. 'I'm going swimming.'

'No, you're not,' I said.

He pulled a rolled-up towel out from his rucksack, looking pleased with himself.

'You'll freeze to death,' I said.

He peeled off his clothes; he was wearing his swimming trunks underneath. Ella stood watching him. Once he was waist high in the water, she took off her coat and pulled up her sweater, revealing a black sports swimming costume. She kicked out of her jeans and pulled a towel from her backpack, which she left on a rock with her clothing. She followed him out, speeding away from us like an otter.

'Nutters,' Tess said.

I dipped my fingers in the water. 'Like ice.'

They were far out in moments, their heads becoming small, slick dots. We watched Christopher turn and wait for Ella to swim up to him. They bobbed within a foot of each other. I briefly wondered what words were being exchanged, before I remembered there would be none.

They took a long time out there, appearing to just tread water. 'I wouldn't in a million, billion years. Not if you paid me,' Tess said.

It began to seem like they were stationary objects that had always been there, like I had imagined them swimming out in the first place. Tess and I started to jump up and down to keep warm. A sharp wind bit at us. Slowly, their heads moved back towards shore, two otters following each other.

When they were within a few metres, they rose out of the water, grinning, clutching their shoulders, dashing the short distance to their discarded clothes. The pebbles must have hurt their feet. I stepped forward and handed Ella her towel. Christopher grabbed his and wrapped it round himself. Tess and I took a wander along the shore while they changed back into their clothes.

. . .

It was uncomfortable for me to admit I didn't like Christopher's girlfriends. Bound up with my feminism was an undefined sense that I should be able to connect to most women. Each of his past partners had been pretty and clever, and they usually had plums in their mouths. I found them spiteful but questioned my judgement. Did I envy their beauty, their place in my friend's life? Was I annoyed that they obviously weren't embarrassed by the private educations they'd mostly had? Or perhaps I fell into a pattern with them, each of us being wary of the other, giving off unfriendly, nervous signals. When I went over their behaviour, though, I always came back to the conclusion that they just weren't nice people. Each time there was a string of little acts or comments that I could only interpret as mean-spirited. I decided Christopher had a knack for finding unpleasant women in the way that some people have a talent for hooking up with cruel men.

After the walk, we had dinner, Christopher made a curry, and then we sat by the fire. We opened a bottle of rum and kept pouring out small measures into coffee mugs. We got onto playing charades; we had our own version of it with our own categories. I thought that Ella might join in, it seemed the ideal activity for her, but she didn't. Instead, she sat on one of the armchairs with her legs folded under her, a closed book of poetry in her small hands. I tried to think the best of her, but I didn't like it when she smiled without saying anything. It felt like she was laughing at me, or Tess. Not long into the game, I noticed that she was swaying slightly. Her eyes were half shut. I kept glancing back at her. I'd seen her take barely a sip of the rum, but, yes, she must be drunk. We carried on with the game, and she seemed to fall asleep, tucking her head against her folded arm on the edge of the couch.

The game fell apart. We argued over the rules, whether objects in the room could be used as clues. Tess was finally declared the winner, gloating, pouring more rum into her mug, seeming to be untouched by it.

'Put some music on,' Christopher said.

I closed my eyes and pulled a CD out of a collection by the fireplace. It was some classical music that wasn't familiar to me at the time, *Danse Macabre* by Camille Saints-Saëns. Initially discordant, it became lively and quick. Christopher took my hands and spun me round on the carpet in front of the fire. The flames had overheated one side of my face so the other felt cold. Tess joined in, and the three of us danced in a circle. We were trying to make each other laugh with increasingly silly moves, playing invisible violins. I saw that Ella was awake, looking at us, so I broke out of the trio to grab her hands and pull her up. She beamed. She danced with me, then Christopher, then me again, but she was rocky on her feet. I could see what was going to happen before it came about. Her heel caught the stone corner of the fireplace. She fell sideways. Although it could only have taken a second, I somehow had time to imagine her falling into the flames, the white flare and terror of it. In reality, she landed in front of the fire, reaching out and grabbing a glowing log that had rolled partially onto the hearth. She made a startled cat noise and sat up clasping her hand.

'Shit, shit,' Tess said.

'Did you burn yourself?' I asked uselessly.

Christopher knelt beside her and tried to take hold of her hand, but she wouldn't let him. 'I'm sorry, I'm sorry, I'm sorry,' he was saying though he hadn't caused it in any way.

We helped her over to the couch. Her hand didn't look too bad, the skin only slightly pink. Though I knew from experience nasty burns could form slowly. Tess nipped to the kitchen and came back with a box of orange ice lollies that must have been left behind by other visitors. She gave one to Ella to hold. We stood round silently, chewing on our lips.

I remembered something then about ice being bad for a fresh burn. 'Wait. You're supposed to hold it under the tap. Ice is too cold.'

We all bundled through to the kitchen. Christopher turned on the faucet, and Ella held out her hand under the flow of water.

'You've got to keep it there for about twenty minutes. I did this once when I picked up a hot baking tray. It feels like forever, but it really makes a difference,' I said.

Ella held herself there by the sink, looking down at the water. Christopher stood behind her and wrapped his arms round her midriff and put his chin on her shoulder. He kissed her neck. Tess and I slipped back through to the sitting room.

'That wasn't your fault,' Tess said.

'I know.' But my face was burning hot on both sides now, like I was ashamed of something.

Later, Tess and I were sipping coffee in front of the television. Christopher and Ella had gone to their room. I got up to find crisps, and while I was in the kitchen, I thought I heard someone leave. The front door opening and bumping closed. After a moment, Christopher came through.

'Where is she?' he said.

'Who?'

'Ella. She just walked out.'

'I heard the door go,' I said. 'She might be in the garden.'

We went to the front step. I could see a figure in a light top disappearing up the road.

'Is she alright?' I said.

'We were fine. Her hand seemed OK. Then she just left.'

'But is she upset?'

'I don't know.'

'I'll go after her,' I said. 'Let me go. I feel a bit responsible.'

I grabbed my coat. Christopher stood back as I made my way out the front door. I sprinted down to the road, the surface shining slick after the rain. Ella was a good distance away to the right, her pale cream top standing out against the tarmac. I called her name, but she carried on walking ahead. I jogged after her. The night air smelt of rain on peaty ground.

As I drew near, she turned to face me but continued to walk away, stepping backwards. 'Is everything OK?' I said.

I knew she wouldn't talk, but I thought she might nod or shake her head. Instead, she kept backing away, her shoulders squared with mine, her eyes on me. 'Are you upset about what happened?' Her expression was neutral; I saw no sign of distress. 'Look, I don't want to pester you. If you want a walk, go ahead. I'll tell Christopher you're getting some air.' No response. Around us, the shapes of the countryside were still recognisable. Though the moon was behind a cloud, it shone bright as a torch through a thin curtain.

Ella did an odd thing then. A distance from me, she stopped and sat down in the middle of the road.

'You'll get wet,' I said. She looked up at me, features unmoving. 'Of course, if you're not bothered about getting wet, why would it matter?' I found myself pausing for her to speak, but naturally she didn't. I put my hands in my pockets. 'Fine. I mean, I'm not going to tell you what to do. You're an adult. But a car could come suddenly.' I felt words winding up and falling out of me. She looked around about her, patted the road as if the pitted surface fascinated her. 'Look, I don't know if you're angry or you're playing a game. I just can't tell. Maybe I'm not that good at reading people. Do you want me to help in any way?' She leant back on her hands and looked at me. Was she just drunk?

'OK, I think I'm going to head back. I'll let Christopher know where you are, though.'

She gave me no reaction, so finally I turned. I could see the window lights from the cottage shining out into the garden. The scene looked like a book jacket for a murder mystery. I began walking back towards the lit garden.

I found the longer I was outside, the sharper my night vision became. I could pick out all the little dints and dips in the tarmac ahead. A patchy hedge ran to the right of me, last years' dead leaves still gathered underneath. The more I could make out, the more I scanned for movement. Twitching branches made me flinch. It was daft, I was in a perfectly safe place, but my eyes flicked from side to side. I tried to focus on figuring out how to describe to Christopher what Ella had done.

A noise, light tapping behind me. Footfalls. A small spasm went through my shoulders, and I turned to look. Ella was up on her feet, following me, just a few paces back.

'Yeah, OK,' I said. 'Yeah, sure. Probably a good idea to head back, it is getting cold.' I tried to keep my voice steady like this was all ordinary.

I kept ahead, she stayed to the back of me. We reached the stone wall boundary of the garden, and I swung the metal gate. I didn't say anything to her. When I walked through the front door, she was six inches behind me. Warmth and light spilled over us. Christopher smiled. He strode across the room and hugged her wordlessly. I didn't say anything about her sitting on the road. I was tired, my eyes beginning to sting.

She and Christopher returned to their room. Tess was still watching the television. I made myself a hot chocolate and looked at the moon through the kitchen window. As I stirred in the cocoa powder, I remembered something I'd heard once, I think on a television programme, about swans mistaking wet roads for rivers. They land on them and sit in a state of confusion, unable to understand why they're not swimming.

The next day, Tess and I went on a hike while Christopher and Ella stayed around the cottage. We followed a track beside a river. The water was high and foaming. We talked for a while about our jobs. I was trying to find new work, applying for one thing after another with no luck. Tess was employed by a homelessness charity.

'How's your funding?' I asked her.

'Looks like we'll squeak through for another year.'

'Good.' I watched the water churning. 'Do you ever get people with speech problems?'

'What like?'

'Mute people?'

'Not exactly. There was one guy who didn't speak when he first came to us. He'd just have the lunch, make gestures for food. After a while, he began to say a few words, *please* and *thank you*. Then he began to say sentences. It wasn't like he was shy. It was like a child learning to talk. You could see him searching for the words. I think that was a brain thing though, a stroke or injury.' She stopped and turned to the river. 'It's funny, isn't it?'

'Must be some kind of trauma for her not to speak at all? You'd know more than me.'

'Hardly. But yeah, I suppose so. Something must have happened.' We carried on walking. 'Now you've made her even more traumatised by pushing her in a fire.'

I shoved Tess almost into the water. 'Shut up. It's not funny. I feel awful.'

In the evening, I waited for a turn of the bathroom. Ella was in there, the shower chattering away. I paced to the door and back several times. Finally, after about fifty minutes, the room was empty. I locked myself in. A window was open, but steam still lingered. When I pulled back the curtain of the shower cubical, the basin was streaked with scummy black lines. As if someone had marked it with charcoal. I wondered if it was dirt from her swim in the loch. Maybe she hadn't washed since then. Scowling, I wiped the plastic with a bundle of damp toilet paper. I must have been pulling a face when I returned to our bedroom because Tess said, 'What is it?'

'Nothing. Just the shower wasn't exactly clean.'

'Was it full of feathers?'

'Something like that.'

Tess made pasta for dinner. Afterwards, we drank wine and played dominos. Christopher, Ella and I arranged ourselves on the floor. Tess sat on the couch behind us and plucked at Christopher's hair, curling and uncurling a lock of it. Ella didn't join in the dominos, though it was another game that required no words. Instead, she watched every movement. I'd given up trying to say things to her. The words only seemed to drop down and lie in the space between us. She'd observe me speaking as if she was watching leaves fall from a tree, and no response was expected.

At about eleven o'clock, while Christopher and Ella withdrew to their room, Tess and I stayed up to flick through the television channels. The embers of the fire had shrunk to resemble miniature torchlights on a dark mountainside. People out searching for a monster. I sat at the far end of the couch while Tess stretched across it with her shins resting on my thighs. Every so often, I poked her feet. When the three of us had been in student halls together, we had draped ourselves over each other like puppies in a basket. I hadn't done that with Christopher in a long time. Gradually it had come to seem sexual in way it absolutely hadn't when we were students. I hardly touched him these days except to kiss him on the cheek if one of us was going away for a long time.

Tess poured herself more wine and whispered, 'He better watch out with his mute swan. They mate for life.'

'Do they? I guess that's something people like to believe because swans look so romantic. The heart-shaped necks and all that.'

'No, no, it's true. There's one on the canal near me. The woman in the canal centre says his mate is missing, but he won't take another because he hasn't seen her body. Isn't that the saddest fucking thing? He has to see her dead before he'll love again.'

'That's awful.'

'I know. I keep seeing him on his own gliding about like a paper boat.'

'Maybe Ella is his escaped mate, turned human,' I said.

'Like in Swan Lake.'

'Except this would be a swan changing into a woman, not a woman turning into a swan.'

'You know, it all adds up.' Tess widened her eyes in pretend shock. 'That's why she's good at swimming. And why she can't speak. Or play games.'

'Or hold her drink.'

We both started giggling.

'I can't believe what we've uncovered,' Tess said.

'We'd better get her back to the canal,' I said. 'Put everything right.'

'She doesn't look like a swan, though, does she? You'd expect a swan to be like a ballet dancer. Tall and thin and graceful.'

'Not necessarily. Real swans are short with wee round bodies, and they waddle along when they're on land.'

Behind us then, there was a tiny scuffing noise. We craned our necks. Someone was walking away through the corridor, the steps too light to be Christopher's. I bit my hand.

'Shit. We're such jerks,' Tess said. We began laughing again, breathless gulps.

'Do you think she heard?'

'I think she did.'

I shook myself and pushed Tess's feet onto the floor. 'I'll go see.'

I hurried along the corridor. She was at the far end. The door to their bedroom was closed. I dashed up behind her, nearly skidding on the floor tiles. She turned to look at me. That long, thin nose and those dark berry eyes. 'I'm sorry,' I said. 'We weren't really talking about you. We were just speculating about fairy tales, magical animals, that kind of thing.' My brain was puzzled and heated with wine and wouldn't offer me the right words. Standing so near her, I caught two scents at once, a woman's perfume and also that faint smell that I'd noticed in the car. It was an outdoorsy odour, of damp vegetation. I looked down. My palm had a row of fading dimples where I had sunk my teeth. For a moment, I had a sense the damp smell was coming from me or my clothes. When I looked up again, Ella was still facing me. She was silent, and then, at last, not silent. The tiniest noise, made with her teeth and lips. I swear it was a hiss. Maybe I projected that onto her, thinking of swans, but that's exactly how I hear the sound now when I replay it in my memory. *Hiss.*

I stepped back. 'OK, alright, I'll leave you alone,' I said. She turned and opened the door to her and Christopher's room and disappeared inside.

When I woke in the morning, Tess was still asleep, twisted in her duvet. I ambled through to the kitchen and found Christopher alone. He was standing in his T-shirt and shorts, holding a carton of milk.

'Where's Ella?' I asked.

'She's gone,' he said.

For one cold moment, for a reason I can't now fathom, I thought he was saying she had died.

'Gone?'

'She's off home,' he said. His tone was flat.

'Oh. Why?'

'I don't know.'

'You saw her leave?' I asked.

'No. She was gone when I woke. She sent me a text.'

Without thinking, I said, 'She can text?'

'Of course she can. She's not fucking illiterate, Claire.'

'Sorry. I didn't mean that. I wasn't thinking.'

Though in truth, as I stood there, I was surprised. I suppose I had begun to imagine her completely cut off from words. I thought back to when I spoke to her. Without defining it, I'd had the sense she didn't actually understand me, like I wasn't speaking her language. 'I hope she's OK. How did she get back?'

'A taxi.'

'A taxi will have cost her a fortune.'

'Yeah, she must have really wanted to get away,' he said. He looked at me solidly. I turned to the cupboard and picked out a cereal bowl.

'That's up to her, I suppose,' I said. 'I'm sorry if things aren't going well.'

We were not a talkative party heading back in the car. Christopher, in the passenger seat most of the way, looked out the window and drummed his fingers on the door. Slivers of snow stood out in the gullies on the far hillslopes, like white shadows where the sun had not reached. Tess played some electro-swing music until I asked her to turn it off.

We did not meet Ella again; she and Christopher didn't get back together.

Tess rang me a few weeks after we arrived home. 'You know what?'

'What?' I said.

'The swan's returned.'

'Which swan?'

'The one on the canal, the missing mate. The female. She was alive all this time.'

'I wonder what happened to her?'

'Who knows? It's a bit suspicious, isn't it?' Tess said. 'Ella disappears off the scene, and the swan is back.'

We laughed.

'Maybe we were right,' I said. 'She was a bewitched swan all along.'

'It is a bit spooky though, eh? I just caught a glimpse of them sailing along together.'

Tess and I went walking on the canal path later that afternoon to look for the pair of swans. The water was dark between the narrowboats and under the bridges. We couldn't find either of them.

'Maybe you imagined it. Maybe it was a large gull. Or a plastic bag.'

'Piss off. I know what I saw.'

We strolled a couple miles up the path, seeing moorhens and coots, clumps of blackthorn blossom and a floating stiletto heel, but we didn't glimpse the pair of swans. We took more walks by the water over the coming weeks as the daffodils burst out. We never saw them. In fact, Tess didn't catch sight of either the male or the female again, though she walked on the canal more or less every day.

The next spring, a pair of swans were back on the water, sailing along, poised as ice carvings. But the woman at the canal centre said they were new, younger birds. She'd never seen the mate return and assumed that the old male had been usurped or had died off quietly somewhere out of sight.

Lighthouse

I have a little daydream about you and I, that we are the last people left on earth, and we live in a lighthouse. We are situated in the far north, the sea around us is the colour of a Russian blue cat. The building has three levels. We have filled the lower storeroom with canned goods and bottled water, with bags of porridge oats and powdered milk, whatever we could find on the journey. Early on, we unearth rods and reels from the cupboard on the stairs. We plan to fish because we know the store won't last forever. I show you how to cast a lure since you never fished as a child.

For the first week, we catch nothing. One morning my fishing rod arks; something large is hooked and moving away. I don't know what to do; I never got as far as landing a catch before. I turn to call to you, and as I do, my hand catches on the unspooling cord. I lose the fish, and I'm left with a red streak across my palm like a worm under the skin. You help me to bandage my hand.

We each miss our partners, of course. You miss your children. But we don't know that we are the last; we cradle a hope of being reunited with them all.

We learn how to prepare the fish, to descale and gut. We become quick with the knife, lose our distaste for the work.

We give titbits to the seagulls who gather on the inner wall. We soon have a favourite bird, he wears a blue ring. Someone tagged him once. We give him extra. For water, we collect rain in buckets and refill used bottles.

We try to make the lighthouse like a home. We turn sack-cloth into curtains. We create a table out of wooden pallets. One day you pick miniature white flowers from the rocks and put them in a mug as a table centrepiece. There is a generator powered by a small wind turbine. Most of the time, we use an electric radiator for warmth, shutting ourselves in the room we call the office. We also burn driftwood in the fireplace, a kind of treat for cold nights. On those occasions, we sit either side of the fire, and you tell me about your children. You try to carve things for them from driftwood, but you feel you're not very good at it. You usually throw the piece in the flames before it has taken on a real shape.

We give the seagull a name; we call him Gregor after a dog you had once. He becomes less nervy than the others, learns to stay close, even when we are noisy.

You and I sleep in the same bed for warmth. Inevitably, we end up making love some nights. We do not discuss it in the daytime. It doesn't feel like a betrayal of our partners because ordinary life has been paused, or stopped.

The winter closes in. The light is short, each span of day like a sliver of butter melting. The heater is no longer enough to keep the main room warm, and we come back from fishing with raw, grazed hands.

'What will we do?' you say.

'We can only carry on,' I say. We burn pallets, packing crates, all the wood we can find, our table last. Ice permanently covers the inside of the window on the stairs. We don't see Gregor over the winter; we fear that he has died.

During those elongated nights, you turn away from me because I want your approval so much. We continue to share a bed, and in the dark we still have sex sometimes, but when we reach the point of sleep, you turn your shoulder blades to me. The more you meet me with silence, the more I try to impress you. I find a tin of black paint at the back of the store cupboard. I make pictures as best I can on the stairwell walls. They look a bit like cave paintings. Outlines of creatures galloping. I make an effort to stay clean, to keep my hair tidy. You sit up late writing letters to your partner and your children, scrawlings that can't be sent anywhere. I rise before you and cook your porridge oats with powdered milk and boiled water. You ignore me. Eventually, I cease trying. I stop speaking and offer you averted eyes instead.

Bit by bit, this tactic brings you back to me. You try to get my attention, the way a pony will come and nuzzle your shoulder if you stand in its field with your back turned. You wash up my dishes on occasion, make extra cups of instant coffee and leave them at the top of the stairs for me to notice.

The problem is I have come to dislike you now because why shouldn't I, when you rejected my efforts first? I begin to spend time with the lightless lamp at the top of the tower. Even unlit, it looks to me like it has been designed by angels.

While the stair window is still iced with winter, we have our biggest argument. You accuse me of enjoying being trapped in the lighthouse, of almost wishing us here. I deny it. 'Everything I love is gone – you have the thing you want most,' you say. I deny that too. (Was there a time before the lighthouse when I'd have gladly lived the life of a dog if that meant sleeping on the floor at the end of your bed? If there was, I would not tell you). After the shouting is done, you go out to the rocks to fish though the weather is wild, the waves breaking in thick foam over the land. Once you are out at the farthest point, I see only your scarlet lifejacket through the spray. I keep going to the window, checking you're still there, minute by minute. One time I look, you are gone.

I run out onto the rocks. At first, I don't see you. Then a glimpse. You are in the water, pitched about by the waves like a red leaf. I dash back to the lighthouse and grab the lifesaver ring from the wall. I clamber out as close to you as I can. I'm shouting to you, but my voice is whipped away. I throw as far as I'm able. The lifesaver doesn't land anywhere near you and quickly washes back in, snagging on a rock almost at my feet. Amongst the waves, I see your face. Your features are sharp, your mouth screaming. I throw the ring again, harder this time. It falls closer, but it misses your reach. You are gulping air, head back, hair slick.

I throw a third time, and you catch. I pull, you move towards me. It takes all my strength. My chapped and plastered hands burn against the rope. I draw you closer, closer. Finally, you crawl ashore gasping, your hands clutch my ankles, my shins. I raise you up. We run inside, and you shed your clothes, and I light the fire with some driftwood, a secret portion I have been saving. You sit wrapped in an old tartan blanket drinking hot tea. I offer you powdered milk, but you refuse it. You sip your bitter drink, and you thank me.

The spring comes edging round. The weather soothes itself. Things settle between us. You bring flowers in again one day, they have tiny purple petals this time and look like violet suns. They are called Thrift, you say. I make a soup out of limpets. You kick them off the rocks since I can't bear to; for reasons I don't understand, it feels crueller than other things. Gregor returns, and we greet him as an old friend. He talks to us in gull language, wagging his head, begging with his pointed tongue. We feed him fish guts. You gather enough driftwood to begin a new table. We knot together crab fishing lines, and they work beautifully, and I mash the sweet white meat into what's left of the tinned vegetables for variety's sake. We glue the shells to the stairwell wall as decoration. We discuss eating birds but dismiss the idea for now. You gather seaweed and set it drying – we don't know which types are good to cook, but you say you will experiment.

This spring is the real start of it all. We begin the work of learning to truly understand each other. It is a joyful season.

Well. This is a daydream I have about the two of us from time to time. It plays through my mind in tranquil moments. When I am working late in the office, or on a train passing by the sea, or when my partner is telling me a long story.

I've written it all down. At this moment, you might be sound asleep or pacing your upstairs landing watching the dawn creep over the wallpaper. Perhaps you are shushing one of your children, trying to coax them back to bed. The seagulls you complain about must be squabbling again in their rooftop nest. I imagine your beautiful face marked with a frown. I have not sent my daydream to you yet because I worry you will not be pleased.

Pipistrelle

An Introduction

One of my clearest and brightest childhood memories is of seeing a sedge warbler up close. I can still picture its tiny, clasped feet, delicate, striped head and flashy cream eyebrow. Growing up in the centre of a large city, it marked my first significant encounter with nature. The bird was held by Arthur Treilan, a look of concentration on his face as he read the ring number. Before releasing it, Arthur allowed me to reach out and stroke the warbler's underside. Though I touched the bird's breast as lightly as I could, I was able to detect a rapid heartbeat against the pad of my finger.

I have debated with myself about how personal this introduction ought to be. In the end, it felt wrong to merely write a detached evaluation of *Pipistrelle*. The book is, like most good nature writing, as much about humans as it is about wildlife. Its chapters are woven through with their author's quirks and passions. It is only secondarily a book about bats. I want to use this space to give a sense of Arthur Treilen not just as a naturalist but as a person. Both the rough and the smooth. It is an opportunity to depict him as something other than a tragic figure, a man who disappeared.

My encounter with the sedge warbler took place forty-two years ago. I was on a week-long break in the west highlands, organised by a charity for 'disadvantaged young people'. We were a group of ten boys, Arthur was on hand as a local expert. Though not bound to, he visited us every day to lead us on nature walks and draw us into conversation. We had no idea at the time that he was already becoming well known for his wildlife writing and radio broadcasts. We were simply magnetised by his enthusiasm.

He taught us that from the earliest moments out of the eggshell, a red grouse chick instinctively pecks at objects which contrast with the background. 'You should aim to do the same thing when you look at a natural landscape – search for divergence, ripples, disparities. That's where the rewards are.' He was also fond of saying, 'The plainer the bird, the prettier the song,' and he'd claim this thinking could be applied to many areas of life.

Arthur invited us back to his home several times during that week. He was then living on the top floor of a Victorian manse on the outskirts of the village, where he had gathered numerous relics, including feathers, hollowed-out eggs, dried scats, and plaster casts of animal tracks. We were allowed to pick up and touch objects from the collection while his then wife Elizabeth Grey, the landscape photographer, brought us tea in thin, china cups as if we were Arthur's adult colleagues. I was unused to being treated with such respect. Arthur's knowledge and generosity that week thrilled something in me and set me down a road that was to lead to my study of zoology at university and eventually to the career I have now. Without his influence, my life could easily have diverged along a bleaker trail, into different woods altogether.

At the end of that first summer, I wrote a letter to Arthur and received a reply from him and Elizabeth inviting me to stay for three nights the following July. So it was that in my teenage years, a custom formed where I spent a long weekend with the couple each summer, or sometimes during the Easter break. These were among the happiest days of my life, though I don't doubt that I was a handful. Arthur was fascinating, Elizabeth was motherly and kind. There were many lessons I learned then that stayed with me. I remember one April visit when I plucked a bullfinch's nest from a hedgerow to show Arthur. Three perfect, speckled, turquoise eggs were cushioned inside on a layer of fine roots. I brought the nest up the manse stairs, into the hallway, cupping it in both hands. When Arthur saw what I held, he shouted at me with such hot rage that I could have turned and run clean out of my own skin. I left the nest on the floor and cowered for the rest of the day, a kicked pup. But I learned then and there to respect nature's property. Birds' nests belong to birds.

Though he could be warm-tempered, he was generous with his time. One day I admitted that I was dumbstruck around a particular girl at my school. 'She wants you to listen to her, not just ramble on in her direction,' he told me. Obvious stuff but revelatory to me at that age to think my inarticulacy might be an advantage. He gave me pointers for my biology homework. 'Don't confuse the how questions with the why questions. *How does the heart beat* is another matter altogether from *why does the heart beat.*' I began to see the subject as an unfolding set of mysteries.

Through various circumstances, and because of a certain kind of chaos at home, I ended up spending one Christmas with Arthur and Elizabeth when I was sixteen. Arthur was a natural heathen and didn't go in for much in the way of

Christmas traditions. Nor did Elizabeth, though she had planned a roast pork dinner with potatoes and trimmings. When I woke late on Christmas morning, I found that Arthur had already set out on a long hike. The land around the house was white with fresh, crumbly snow, the kind that only seems to fall in childhood, though I was at the tail-end of it by then. Elizabeth and I spent the afternoon playing cards and looking through her most recent photographs, with her describing what she thought were the flaws or merits of each image. I remember the light from the fire gave Elizabeth the appearance of a Grecian sculpture. She was a beautiful woman, though not in an immediately obvious way. In the evening, because Arthur had not arrived, we refrigerated the dinner and ate cheese sandwiches and listened to the radio. Arthur had apparently gone visiting, and he did not come back until near ten at night. With his return, we had the Christmas dinner cold from the refrigerator, the uncurtained windows dark beside us. A branch of holly sat in the middle of the kitchen table; Arthur had brought it back with him. The three of us sat eating off willow-patterned plates, our faces flushed from laughter and fullness. Arthur downing the brandy like it was water, completely unaffected by it. If Elizabeth was offended by his wanderings, she did not show it.

At university, I found other ways to pass my summers, and my winter breaks were spent in halls with a number of international students. But I kept up with Arthur's writing and his new television series. I sent him a handful of letters which he usually replied to within a few weeks, penning a short note on the back of a dog-eared wildlife postcard.

Finally, as a doctoral candidate, I returned to Arthur's village, buck-toothed and overeager. He had done well out of his television programmes by this stage, but he had separated from Elizabeth. As he was not the most forthcoming of men, I can only imagine how hard that was. Truth be told, I missed her calming presence, and I still occasionally corresponded with her by letter. For the rest of her life, she sent me a Christmas card. I did not stay with Arthur this time around. Instead I rented a room above the post office shop in the main street. However, he included me on many of his adventures. Long hill climbs to spot golden eagles, patient otter stake-outs in a remote lochside hide. My passion and focus of study then was marshland birds, and we spent many hours picking trails through low, boggy ground.

He began writing *Pipistrelle* around that time. He explained it to me as an account of childhood mixed with a natural history of bats. There is much of the boy becoming enthralled by nature in the book. My experience with the sedge warbler is mirrored by a section in which Arthur describes finding a bat crawling on the floor of his grandparents' attic as a five-year-old child. *'I was captivated by the movement, so alien and unlike any other creature I knew. The winged arms pulled the slight, furred body across the surface of the wood, the animal's pig-face twitching constantly. A martian or bottle imp would have interested me less. The joy it created in me was hard to contain.'* Reading the part where he helps himself to some blackbirds' eggs brings me a wry smile. He kept the shells on his windowsill because there was no nature-loving adult to shout at him.

He told me the writing process gave him comfort. He found 'snatches and gaps around the witching hour', allowing him to write small sections of memory or do a little research.

By this time, Arthur had moved from the drafty apartment in the manse to an even draftier two-story house half a mile out of the village. His collection of nature artefacts had gained its own room. Shelved from floor to ceiling, there were still some empty spaces for new finds. He said these waiting gaps gave him a sense of anticipation. Living with him then was a research student named Diana Greenlaw, who later became a renowned bird artist. Dressed habitually in plain grey overalls, at that time she was experimenting with rapid ink and watercolour sketches, often working long hours outside. I must declare some interest here as Diana was to go on to be both a collaborator of mine and, much later, my wife. I was once laughably described as a 'love rival' of Arthur's in a profile piece written by a journalist who had completely misunderstood a comment of mine. Diana's relationship with Arthur was certainly over when ours began. At that time in the village, I saw her only as a friend. She and Arthur would vanish on long foraging trips together, bringing back mushrooms, blaeberries or wild garlic. They shared almost a secret language from which I was rightly excluded.

I have many memories of that period. Discoveries, miniature breakthroughs, simple pleasures like listening for the first cuckoo of spring. I would often meet Arthur walking alone at night. I'd head out for air or to stargaze. Wandering along surrounded by the soft patter of rain, thinking I was the only human soul abroad, I'd see a thin beam of torchlight hobbling down the road towards me. At times he was out with night vision equipment observing bats, on other occasions he was just walking. He joked about being able to see in the dark with his naked eye because of all the carrots his nanny made him eat as a boy. He said in all seriousness that the night air did something for his spirit. He had an ability to go into an intense state of concentration. I remember seeing him one evening, a few metres up ahead, leaning on an arched stone bridge, peering into the water. I called out so as not to startle him.

He didn't respond, but I assumed he'd heard me. When I was right next to him, I said his name. He jumped round like an adder had bitten him. Straightening himself, he told me he hadn't heard me at all. When I asked what he had been fixating on, he paused then said, 'Bats.' There were none around the river that night, so these creatures must have existed in his mind's eye only.

Arthur was never dull, and that meant there were some turbulent moments. I borrowed his night-vision goggles one evening in June, and they somehow ended up with water damage. No doubt carelessness on my part. We had an argument about what was at that time a very expensive piece of kit. We each lost our tempers to a rather silly degree, and we were embarrassed about it later.

There followed some tension over a stray cat which Diana had named Tabby. The cat would mew loudly at the back window, and Diana would secretly bring it small lumps of cheese. One day Diana let the cat in through the sliding garden door. When Arthur saw it, he said nothing but simply picked it up by the scruff of the neck and carried it back outside. Arthur did not have much patience for animals as domestic pets. Soon, every time Arthur was out, Diana would let the cat in, and every time Arthur came home, he would snatch the cat from its place on the countertop, carry it into the back garden and deposit it on the far wall. It was a source of strain but also humour between Diana and Arthur. It's fair to say they both took their relationship quite lightly. Diana returned to her parents' home later that summer, taking the cat with her in a travel basket, and didn't come back.

It was years later that I met Diana again, one rainy day on a London street. When she and I did eventually marry, Tabby was still going strong. A tough old creature, he became a much-loved pet with our children and lived to be at least eighteen.

Arthur's fame began to grow following the broadcast of a second television series on nocturnal British wildlife. The attention sometimes brought problems, and he never acclimatised to it. While I was back staying in the village, a newspaper article wounded him deeply. The report talked about him getting drunk and being at the centre of a number of blazing rows in the village pub. He suspected someone local of giving the story to the press. He told me it was entirely fabricated, and in all the years I knew him, I never saw him overindulge during the day as the article claimed.

But it is true that not everyone liked him locally. One evening out walking, the two of us came across a dead hen harrier. Together we examined it: its marbled, chocolate chest and masked face. No sign of blood or injury. Arthur took out some plastic sheeting from his rucksack and wrapped the bird up. 'Poisoning,' he said. 'I'll pass it on to a friend who can test it and send the results to the police.'

We ran into the landowner a few days later. A hulk of a man who often drove with a rifle diagonally across the passenger seat. He slowed his car next to us and wound down the window. 'Heard you found a dead harrier up by the coffin route?' he said. Arthur confirmed that we had. The landowner suggested there was no point in Arthur wasting time or money getting the bird tested. Arthur politely said that he couldn't think of a better way to spend either. The landowner's face was grim. He wound up his window. After we walked on past, Arthur gave in to a narrow smile.

The results came back indicating the bird had been poisoned with a common carbonate pesticide. The dose meant it was likely to have eaten meat illegally adulterated. This information and the little corpse were forwarded to the police. Nothing came of it. Arthur received anonymous letters telling him not to stick his snout in other people's business. But he did it every time he found a dead raptor. In the end, there was a prosecution. A gamekeeper was sent to prison for six months for poisoning ravens, which must have saved a number of birds and made Arthur a few extra enemies. One day I saw him with a purplish bruise at the side of his left eye. I asked him what had happened. He laughed. 'Someone doesn't like my keen eyesight,' he said.

After my doctorate was complete, I left for England and didn't see Arthur often, but I watched all his programmes and kept in touch again by letter and, later, by email. Whenever I was in the area, we would meet up. I always found him warm, but it can be said he struggled with human company. Throughout his career, there were a number of feuds with broadcasters, publishers and others in his professional field. He liked to visit people individually, but he hated to be in crowded places, amongst concrete and metal. He told me once that he had a recurring nightmare in which he found himself in a city that he couldn't leave. He'd jump on buses, then trains, travelling for miles, but the city continued, high tower blocks shutting out the sky. As the dream rolled on, more people would crowd into his carriage until bodies were pressed up against him. They all had faces like stretched gauze. He'd wake with his legs kicking at the sheets.

In an autobiographical essay written many years after their divorce, Elizabeth described him as aloof. Fair enough, that was her own recollection, but I think a more fitting word might be undomesticated. After Elizabeth's influence was gone, I found his home lost its order. In later years, I noticed he had very few plates and cups. He told me that as crockery broke, he wouldn't replace it because 'two of everything is enough. One for a visitor and one for me.' He made the worst tasting coffee I have ever had and seemed to subsist on shop-bought biscuits at times. He let the garden grow tangled though it had been neatly cultivated when he bought the place. In my latter visits, it was thick with waist-high nettles, and the bird feeding station set up by Diana had rotted apart.

On one occasion, I caught up with him in Liverpool city centre. I was working on a newspaper at the time, and he was visiting an academic. We met in a greasy spoon type café; I'd assumed he wouldn't like anything fussy. It was the busiest time of day; the tight space of the café seemed to keep filling with people buying hot drinks to take away. Sitting across from me, Arthur's expression and demeanour reminded me of an old fox I'd seen. The animal had been trapped in a wire cage so it could receive veterinary treatment. Like the fox, Arthur's eyes flicked around, catching people passing by the window, a rapid movement at the till. I could almost see his ears pricking and twisting. As I began making notes for this introduction, I offered this description to Diana, and she nodded, 'Yes, like a dog fox, I saw that in him too.' He had an intense dislike of anthropomorphism but had no qualms about its reverse. In *Pipistrelle*, he often describes people as animals, their manners or habits, so he might not have disapproved of this description.

For someone who struggled with crowds, it is interesting that he was so drawn to bats, who often live in colonies of thousands. In *Pipistrelle*, a section recounts his trip to Chile to study *Desmodus rotundus*, the vampire bat. He writes with great fascination about their interlinked existence: '*The common vampire bat must feed every other day, or it will die, but if an adult returns to the roost without having fed successfully, its neighbours will regurgitate blood for it just as if it were their own offspring.'*

Eventually, he did start to lose out on programme offers. His reputation for being difficult increased, though I felt this was mainly unfair. When my career was beginning to take off, I got into a heated exchange with a producer about a decision to exclude him from a project. We did manage to do a local television programme together shortly afterwards, and I found him a joy to work with then. There was one moment while we were filming marshland birds, when an incredibly rare sandhill crane, blown off its migration route, landed in front of us. Arthur's face lit up like a boy presented with a chocolate cake.

One summer, about five years before he went missing, he invited me to stay with him at his house, something I hadn't done since those early days. We laughed a lot during that time. Someone had given him an enormous stock of home-made bramble wine with which he was particularly delighted. He began teaching me the basics of taxidermy, but I didn't have the stomach for it.

A few days in, there was a preposterous story on a newspaper's website stating Arthur had been seen threatening me with a knife in a hotel bar. The reality is more mundane. We were having lunch locally, we got into an animated debate about deer cull quotas, and he was waving his steak knife for emphasis. A few sharp words were traded, and he did stand up at one point. I suppose other people were watching us. It was reported that he said, 'I'll cut your voicebox out,' which is true, but this was very much a common figure of speech for Arthur. It didn't mean anything.

However, we had a quiet disagreement a few days later that sadly did lead to a rift. No raised voices, no drama. I genuinely cannot now remember what it was over, though I believe it was to do with a filming project he had in mind that I had doubts about. I left for London the next morning.

There followed a few years when we did not speak, and I now regret that deeply. A couple of times, I wrote a postcard to him and then put it away in a drawer unsent.

We got back in touch eleven months before his disappearance. He initiated contact with a handwritten letter full of lively observations about the spring migration. Typical of Arthur, he did not refer to our disagreement. He illustrated the page with a pencil drawing of a corncrake which I unfortunately cannot now find. I was invited to his house and travelled there in late April. The old joy in seeing him came flooding back to me. I found the garden piled with fencing and chopped wood under tarpaulin, the inside of the house more crammed than ever with nature mementos. Animal skulls and pellets. A newly stuffed stoat in standing position, created from one he'd found killed on the roadside. There were no empty spaces on the shelves now. On the walls were a haphazard collection of wildlife photographs and paintings. And of course, piled everywhere, many, many books. I had brought him a print of a sedge warbler, painted by Diana. 'Stunning,' he said. 'This will get pride of place.' The next day when I came down to breakfast, it was above the fire in the living room. He never said things he didn't mean. He was down to one breakfast bowl now, and so he ate his cereal from a mug while I was there.

These days were the last I saw of him, and I'm glad to say we parted on good terms, Arthur clasping my hand in his rough old palms before I got in my car.

I will not go into sensationalist detail regarding his disappearance, but I cannot leave it out entirely. At first, his postman noticed he was not at home for a number of days. Friends tried to contact him. I was called and initially played it down; Arthur would turn up. Eventually, when it was realised no one had heard from him in weeks, an alarm was raised, and a search began. Diana and I travelled north to see if we could help. His home had been left as if he intended to return to it. There was a dish in the sink, books marked up for further study, a cup of lemon flu remedy half drunk. But the longer we spent searching, the more a dark feeling came over me. There was a point where Diana and I both sat on the stone bridge near his house and wept like lost children.

After he had been missing for three months, newspaper articles hinted at suicide. Some friends wondered if he had simply got tired of the world and hidden himself further away. On the internet, people speculated about murder, which is of course an absurd suggestion. Though he was often willing to ruffle feathers, there was never anything so serious. There were persistent rumours that he had got into a fight with a local publican in the weeks before he vanished, and that the dispute was over his relationship with the pub owner's adult daughter. However, I found this unlikely, firstly because I knew the pub's owner to be a shy, gentle man. Secondly, because Arthur had told me himself that his time for romantic relationships was over. 'I experience solitude like a beautiful drug these days,' he said to me. I tend to find the more persistent rumours are, the less truth there is in them. I even saw my own name mentioned as a possible culprit. At times I think of the internet as a celtic sea serpent eating itself.

Arthur's body was never found, and it took several years before he was formally declared dead. The coroner ruled accidental death, and I personally believe that he came to some misfortune while out in a remote place, perhaps near sea cliffs.

A sudden fall, or health problem. I am certain it was not suicide. He was still buzzing with the joys of life. I don't think he wanted to do anything to hasten its end. I find peace in the idea of his remains resting somewhere wild, as if he'd been given a form of Tibetan sky burial.

If he were still alive today, he would be well into his eighties. Though I believe he is gone, I have often entertained a daydream of walking back into his nature-filled house to be met with his quick smile, a cup of dreadful coffee, and an energetic description of his latest discovery.

I remember him most as he was when we were in wild places together, that quiet concentration. One autumn back when I was still a teenager, we took a dawn hike through a narrow glen and came upon two rutting red deer stags in among a group of hinds. We watched them push each other in circles, their antlers locked. Their breath puffing into the frost-scented air. Arthur said nothing. He saw no need to explain anything about the ecology or mating habits of the deer. We both just crouched there watching, the only sound the clicking of the antlers. The weaker stag was eventually forced backwards, its shoulder torn. When it lost its footing and turned tail, we too turned and began to head back to the village without needing to comment. It was like we both knew we had witnessed something that idle conversation would demean. Though I have observed the rut many times since, it never loses its power to strike me silent.

Pipistrelle is a beautiful account of nature and also of a human life. Like all of Arthur's writing and broadcasting, it sings with a passion for its subject and leads us deeper into reflecting on our place in the animal kingdom. If this volume is an old favourite of yours, I welcome you back to it, and if you are exploring it for the first time, I hope it brings you both pleasure and wonder.

Fingerpricks

'The girls are to go to the gym hall. Boys go on to your next class.'

The girls gathered and flocked down the corridor like geese.

'What's this about?'

'Why's it just us?'

'We're getting fingerpricks. I'll bet you any money.'

'What's that when it's at hame?'

'It's when they jab a needle into your finger to get blood out.'

'Oh, Jesus.'

'Why do they do that?'

'I don't know, it's just what they do. Happened at my last school.'

'How'd you know it's that?'

'Because that's why it's only the lassies. They don't do it to boys.'

'Why not?'

'They just don't.'

'It willnae be that, they cannae give you a jag without asking your parents.'

'They didn't ask at my last school, it just happened one day. A girl fainted in the queue, and they still did it to her when she got back up. They jab a needle into your finger and squeeze it tight so the blood drips out. Look, Shona's gonna faint right now.'

'No, I'm not. I don't believe you. Even if they try to do anything, I'll go home and tell my mum to ring the school and say I'm sick.'

'Listen to how posh she is. *My mum will phone Balmoral and tell the Queen to tell the school to leave her precious, darling daughter alone.* Aye, but she's gone white.'

They filed into the gym hall where the chairs were lined up in higgledy rows at the front. A police officer leant back against the stage, holding her hat in her hand, her hair tied back in a blonde bun. As they took their seats, she straightened up.

'My God, you all look miserable. The faces on you. Have you just come from double maths or something?'

There was no answer.

'I'm here to talk to you today about personal safety.'

'This is cos of what happened to Isla,' someone whispered.

'Maybe we're getting fingerpricks at the end.'

'Shut up, just cos you were wrong, ya numpty.'

'Do you want to share what you're all whispering about?' said the police officer, a pair of handcuffs glinting at her hip.

'Miss, I mean not miss, but officer, we were wondering why the boys aren't here?'

'We don't need the boys. This is a chat between us women.'

It was the first time they'd been called women. The police officer began to speak to them about walking at night.

'Put your house keys between your fingers. You can use them as a weapon if you need to hit someone. Like this.' She took out a fist of keys from one of many pockets and demonstrated. 'Also, show your thumbs, keep them visible. It's a sign of dominance. Don't tuck your hands away in your sleeves when you're nervous. Boys get into trouble when they look too confident – girls get into trouble when they don't look confident enough.'

She took out a pepper spray canister and a personal alarm. The pepper spray looked like a miniature deodorant, the alarm like a shiny-backed beetle. The alarm was so loud, she said, she would not pull out the toggle in the gym hall because it would deafen them all. 'Another thing I want to talk to you about. Women's intuition. Do you know what intuition is?'

Some of the girls thought they knew but didn't say because they did not want to come across as stupid, or clever. A few had never heard the word before. A girl called Ruby wasn't listening. Catherine knew exactly what intuition meant and thought it was patronising to suggest women had a special version of it, but she didn't respond because she never spoke at school from the first bell to the last.

The police officer answered their silence. 'Women get a gut feeling about things sometimes. If a situation doesn't feel good – and I'm saying this because it's more likely to be someone you know, it's not likely to be out on the street – if a situation doesn't feel right, get out of there.' She turned her hat in her hands. The badge on the front was from no Christmas cracker.

'But miss, officer miss, what if you do all that and it still happens to you?'

'Then you phone the police, that's what we're here for.'

'What if the police don't believe you?'

Putting her cap back on, the officer said, 'You will be believed – you always will.'

. . .

What happened to Isla. She was two years above them and into art and drama and all that line of thing. They had looked up to her for her dark sense of humour and detailed knowledge of biology. One October break, a friend of her uncle's who was a photographer of some kind, apparently, invited her round to his flat and took pictures of her. She visited him every week from then on. He'd bring in a Chinese takeaway or iced cakes from the bakers, and shoot pictures of her in different poses. One day he took photographs of her naked except for a fur rug which she wore on her shoulders like a cloak. He said it was for art. 'What a fucking idiot, imagine thinking it was for art,' one of the boys said afterwards. The naked photographs appeared on the internet, and one of the boys found them and printed them out and placed smudged copies around the school like wagging tongues. The photographer was arrested and then released without charge. Isla went to her mum, and her mum went to the press, and so they appeared in the local paper, sitting next to each other on a cream couch that was not their own, Isla's bright stoat eyes peering from the page. 'Schoolgirl claims pervert photographer tricked her.' Some people said that because Isla was sixteen at the time, the whole thing didn't count. Since the newspaper article, Isla hadn't been back to her classes.

'I wouldn't show ma face at school, I'd be too embarrassed,' one of the girls said.

'She's a tart, like her mum,' one of the boys said.

'How do you know about her mum?'

'How d'you think I know?' the boy said.

'In your dreams.'

'On my couch.'

'On your couch, in your wet dreams, in your superman pyjamas.'

Before it all, Isla sometimes taught the younger years drama. Not officially; she was just a helper to the drama teacher Mr Mearns. But he took to sitting on the piano stool at the back of the class, thumbing through a detective novel while Isla stood at the front giving instructions. The boys and girls together, she taught them dance steps, breathing exercises, how to be a caterpillar or a weeping willow tree, all the time acting as if doing these things wasn't ragingly embarrassing. 'I'd rather be dead than pretend to be a fucking willow tree,' they muttered to each other, and then they did it, the girls and the boys, flopping their heads, dangling their skinny arms towards the chewing-gummed floor like branches brushing the surface of an ornamental lake. Isla was large in a way that seemed to free her to take up space. She wore silk scarves and bright trousers instead of the dark jeans and tracksuit bottoms that were almost a uniform. They laughed at her clothes; she looked like a lorikeet that had landed among them on its way back to somewhere hot. She knew the younger children, though, and understood how to soothe them. 'I think it's great that you don't blether on all the time, Catherine, your mind must be whirring away in there.' A small tap to the forehead. Catherine was startled at being spoken to directly; usually both pupils and teachers talked of her in the third person.

'Getting older is about learning to give less of a fuck about what people think of you.' Isla used to say this in a way that implied she had a quarter or half-century on them all. Her breath always smelt of red cherry laces so that her words came out sweetened. For the end of term play, she was Cleopatra, transformed by a straight black wig with a fringe, her eyelids sooty. Mr Mearns had made a musical out of it, penning a ridiculous set of songs, which she sang like a robin on a winter morning up before the bins are taken away. At the curtain call, the younger years whistled, hooted, clapped, giggled as Isla bowed and blinked into the golden stage light.

One of the girls went round to Isla's flat after the episode with the photographs, the only person from the school to see her. The girl reported back that Isla had not spoken much. She had tried to dye her hair auburn, but it had come out pink, a shrimpish colour. She'd spent a while standing by the kitchen window staring out at two squirrels scrabbling on the fence in the shared backgreen. Finally, she'd said, 'I didn't know, I didn't know, I didn't know. I thought it was real.'

No one else saw her after that. Someone wrote a card with a bulldog puppy on it that was posted out but received no reply. A few of the girls thought it was a mistake to choose a bulldog; Isla might think she was being called fat. Months passed, enough time for jokes and stories about her to become more elaborate, to grow fingers and toes, and then for it all to begin to fade, until the memory of Isla herself was vanishing, like a handprint disappearing from a steamed-up window. Now, no one had really added up how long she hadn't been at school, and most of the girls had only remembered about her when they saw the police officer and heard her name whispered. That brought her to the surface of their minds like an early toy unearthed at the back of a wardrobe. The pretending they'd done, the games they'd played. By the time the bell rang for break, when the discussion was over and the police officer was back leaning against the stage, Isla's face and voice had returned to them.

In the playground, the boys watched the girls advance, spilling out and down the steps in their dark clothes.

'What was all that about then?' they asked when the girls reached them.

'Fingerpricks.'

'What's that?' The boys massed around the girls like gulls.

'It's when they jab a needle into your finger to get blood out.'

'Really? Eugh. Nae joy.'

'It's dead sore. They squeeze and squeeze until the blood's dripping.'

'Why'd they do it?'

'They didn't tell us – it's just what they do. If they don't get blood the first time, they jab another finger, then another, then your thumbs.'

'Ha ha. Bet you were all greetin'.'

'None of us cried. You're getting them next by the way.'

'Shut up.'

'They told us to tell you,' said the girls, grinning, rows of pearl teeth. 'They told us to tell the laddies to line up outside the gym hall because they're getting fingerpricks next.'

'Piss off.'

'Three of the girls fainted and when they woke, they did it to them anyway.'

'Yous are all lying. They need a letter to give you a jag.'

'That's what we thought. They said letters don't count anymore. Three girls fainted, and they dragged them back to their feet and got the needles out of the wee plastic packets and jabbed them anyway.'

'Who fainted then?'

'Shona did. And Ruby. And Catherine. They flopped like rag dolls.'

'If they fainted, why are they laughing now?'

'They're laughing because it's the boys next, and they think it's funny.'

'We don't believe you.'

The girls backed together in a circle, facing outwards. 'Doesn't matter. You'll find out. You've all gone pale, by the way. There's the bell.'

Verdict

Robert was reading a newspaper in the conservatory when the young man from court appeared. Standing wordlessly beside the potted ferns and umbrella plants, the young man wore the same baggy suit and blue tie he'd worn in the dock. His name was Connor Boyd, and earlier that afternoon, Robert had sentenced him to three years in prison, to serve at least eighteen months before being considered for parole. Now, Boyd was blocking the door that led into the house. The tail end of an ornate tattoo was just visible on the back of his hand. Without the context of the courtroom, he seemed less bulky but still obviously strong.

There were circular panic buttons placed throughout the house; none had been installed in the conservatory. Robert had mentally rehearsed for a moment like this many times over the years. His planned tactics were to begin a dialogue and to look around for an object that could be transformed into a weapon.

He addressed Boyd with what he had always intended to be his opening line. In a flat, gentle voice he said, 'May I help you?' The young man's eyes were tired, and he did not immediately move or reply.

Placing his newspaper on the side table, Robert glanced at the floor and saw the stick for closing the skylight within reach. He could roll it closer with his left foot if necessary.

He looked up. Boyd was no longer in front of him. He was not anywhere in the conservatory. The empty space pulsed. Behind him in the garden, a wood pigeon was making low, guttural calls to its mate. For a queasy slice of time, Robert imagined Boyd heading into the house where Akari would be, where she was perhaps playing at her electronic piano with her headphones on or immersed in her family emails.

But he would have heard the conservatory door open, the creak of the handle, and the brushing of the storm guard on the tiles. There would have been the clang of the boot-scraper mat as Boyd stepped off it. The conservatory door was closed as if the young man had shut it noiselessly behind himself, though that was not possible.

The door had not been opened or closed at all. Boyd had never been there.

Robert stood up in one rapid movement that created dizzy stars in front of his eyes. He made his way into the house. No one was in the kitchen, just the resting, mute appliances. The kettle, the microwave, the toaster, all glinting harmlessly.

'Akari?' he called up the stairs. No answer. He drew breath and called more loudly. 'Akari!'

'Just a minute, I'm on the phone,' came his wife's voice, un-flustered.

He searched each of the ground floor rooms and found nothing, only the plain, cooling silence of the summer evening. He climbed the stairs and discovered his wife sitting with her feet on the bed, the phone snug against her ear. Giving repeated, staccato nods as she generally did when talking to her sister. The cat was curled like a fur hat beside her.

He searched the other rooms. The cornered shadows contained nothing.

Returning to the conservatory, he sat back down and stretched out his hands and found that his fingertips were trembling. There was perhaps a problem here, maybe more of a problem than if the young man had actually been in the house. He had seen something that wasn't real. For want of a softer expression, he'd been hallucinating. He took his own pulse. Marching beats, just a fraction fast. The beds of his fingernails were a healthy pink. It had been a hot day, but the heat had long receded. The only thing was that his eyes stung slightly – perhaps he'd got sun cream in them – so it felt as if he'd been crying. There were no flaws in his vision that could explain the appearance of the figure. He'd only had one glass of Talisker. He looked around the conservatory, at the butterfly packing cases that had been stored there and never emptied, at the slender bookshelves full of anything except legal manuals, at the floral cabinet where Akari kept her gardening tools. Everything was clear and sharp.

He wouldn't tell his wife straight away so as not to worry her unnecessarily. He would ring the doctor in the morning.

But when the dawn came sifting through, he didn't feel like phoning Dr Turner. The sunrise made the world seem placid and secure. He dozed, and when he got himself downstairs, Akari was already at the table, dipping slices of toast into a runny egg. The cat had his nose to the backdoor, waiting to be let out, flicking his feathery tail.

'I made the posh coffee,' Akari said, not looking up.

Robert went over to the pot and poured himself a cup. To tell her was on the tip of his tongue, the edge of his teeth, but he did not. He sipped his hot coffee, ate, changed, and ordered a taxi to the court.

The day was spent on a single case. It involved accusations of breaking and entering, and theft, against a defendant who was mainly basing her plea on not being the woman in the furry security footage. The technical evidence was tedious, and the courtroom was over-warm. During a break, Robert met with Lib McCullough, a medic he'd known for years. She was in today as an expert witness on a separate case in court four.

They talked for a while about the weather, the unusual, shimmering heat this summer, whether it wasn't actually bad news for the world, though weren't they enjoying it now?

'We've shafted this planet. We're doomed,' Lib said. 'Enjoy your aperol spritz ice lollies while they last.'

He gave a slight smile. He was edging towards asking her about the hallucination. The word doom brought it closer to the surface. He half imagined that once it was out there, someone would appear to whisk him off to a psychiatric hospital. 'What do you know about hallucinations?'

'For a court case?'

'No, actually, something outside.'

'Not very much – it's not my line. Far more common than people think,' she said.

'Ever had one?'

'I once got one of those hypnagogic things. I was in a strange hotel room, and I was frozen to the bed. I saw a figure standing in the doorway of the bathroom. A cross between a rodent and a man.'

'Sounds hideous.'

'Bloody terrifying. I knew it wasn't real. That didn't make it less frightening.' She paused, clicking at her silver pen. 'That's to do with sleep, though, so I suppose it's more in the category of a dream.'

'Well, I think I had my first hallucination yesterday.'

'Seriously?'

He made his voice matter of fact. 'I saw a lad from the court, in my conservatory, except he wasn't really there. He vanished straight away.'

She nodded, the pen clicking slowed. 'Overworked, I would guess.'

'Really? But that isn't enough, is it? I've never seen anything like that before.'

'What happened exactly?'

'I looked up toward the door into the kitchen, and he was there. Someone I'd just sentenced. I looked down for a handy weapon, and he was gone.'

'And nothing else happened?'

'Nothing.'

'And you're alright today?'

'Right as rain.'

'Not sick, not feverish? Not on something?'

'No.'

'Mmm, apophenia.' She raised a finger as she often did when she hit on the word she wanted. 'When the brain fills in the blanks, creates meaning out of disorder. How the knots in a piece of wood become the face of Jesus. You were thinking about this guy all day in court – at home, you glanced up, maybe you saw a jumbled reflection, and your brain fleshed it out.'

'Yes, maybe, yes.' Except it wasn't like that. The image had been so precise. He'd seen the sheen of Boyd's tie, the detailed pattern of the tattoo on the back of his hand. Though, had he?

What was the tattoo? Something tail-like, the tip of a fish or a mermaid?

His break was nearly over. They each gathered up their papers.

'I wouldn't worry. It's the likely explanation if you've got no other symptoms. Go home at the end of the day and have a quiet evening, get some time out in the sun. In the global warming.' Lib stood up to leave. 'If it doesn't happen again, I wouldn't take it too seriously. If it does, or you feel nauseous or dizzy or anything, call your doctor.' She smiled. 'Don't call me, I'll be sunbathing.'

He let the jury go early, at half four, since it was obvious that the case was going to run into a second day. There were grateful murmurings.

He was home by seven. Akari was away at her geology class. She'd likely stay out for a drink afterwards. She'd been retired five years now and said she'd never teach again, only be taught. *I'll soak it all up like a thirsty tomato plant.* He didn't go outside in the evening sun, but he did reconnoitre the conservatory. Empty. He sat down for a moment in the same wicker chair, at an identical angle, and studied the doorway. Yes, there were funny patterns of shade and light. An impressionist print on the far wall of the kitchen, which Akari had bought recently, was also in his line of vision. It was just possible that all this had conspired together to mix the signals in his brain.

He headed back through to the kitchen, where he heated his dinner of chicken and potatoes. Carrying the plate into the living room, he sank in front of the television. He watched a comedy quiz and then a legal thriller. He usually turned off shows like that, but tonight there was a pricking desire to see what happened next. Towards the end of the drama, the lawyer for the main character was alone in her house, still wearing her immaculate work clothes, when a figure from a previous scene appeared behind her. The lawyer did not see him, but the viewer saw the denim of his jeans, the black of his top sliding blurrily into the hallway. Watching this, Robert drew a blanket over his feet. The lawyer was stabbed three times. The theme music began.

It almost made him laugh, the way the scene could have been picked to unnerve him. He switched the television off. Looking around the room, the dark corners were deepened by the knowledge Akari was not in the house. But he was not a child to be spooked by a TV show. The more he thought about it, the more the theory about random patterns made sense.

He read his paper for a while then made his way upstairs to get ready for bed. The house was quiet but in a melancholy, not unsettling, way. Birds singing in the dusk outside. He entered the bedroom and shut the door and in the same moment, saw Boyd standing on the other side of his bed. The young man was wearing the suit and blue tie again. His head was squarish and covered in blonde stubble which caught the light from the overhead lamp. His lips were a little chapped, his hands blue-veined. The tattoo was there. A fishtail? He took a step towards Robert round the side of the bed, his expression neutral, moving as a real man would. Robert stepped backwards, and Boyd stepped forward, and Robert moved again and banged his back against the bedroom door.

'Are you real?' Robert said.

He got no answer. Boyd kept looking at him, the same weary eyes. A thought scurried through Robert's mind: he had been mistaken the night before, Boyd had silently slipped from the conservatory into the house and hidden here all this time. He turned and scrabbled with the door handle, aware the plane of his back was exposed. He got the door open and squeezed out, almost shutting it on himself in his rush to escape.

He banged the door closed and held the handle with all his weight in case Boyd tried to pull on the other side.

'Are you there?' he called. 'Is anyone on the other side of this door?'

Humming silence. He clutched the handle, hurting the pads of his palm. He imagined the door being ripped open by powerful arms. If Boyd was really there, this might be the end of his life.

He listened at the wood panel. There was no noise but his own ears rushing and the chittering of the evening birds. He stayed there, fixed, a long time.

Gradually his mind offered him leeway – the man surely could not have snuck into the house without being heard. Why would he hide for so long, why not strike sleeping bodies in the night if attack was the plan? How in hell could he have got out of prison without anyone reporting it? And though the figure was realistic, something in his gut had told him it had no substance even as he backed away from it. He could try looking. If he pushed the door open and the young man was there, he'd have time to slam it and run.

There was total silence now.

'Is anyone there?' he called. He stood up straight, bracing his feet, and opened the door a sliver.

The bedroom looked empty. Without warning, he flung the door right back so that it hit the wall behind. Empty. He stepped into the room. Hurried round the edge of the bed. Nothing.

Childishly, he lifted the quilt and peered underneath the bed even though he knew the gap was only three inches. He opened the sliding wardrobe, though there wasn't much room to hide there either. He checked his side, piled with work shoes and suits. He checked Akari's side, with her summer dresses and sandals to the front. Empty, nothing. He slid the cupboard shut. In the mirrored panels, his own puzzled face met him, looking elderly and meek. On the wall, there was a chip out of the paint where he'd thumped the bedroom door back.

The room was empty. But this was no slight misperception. The man had been there in full detail, three dimensions. The shadows on his face changing as he moved in relation to the lamp. If it was a hallucination, it was a well-constructed one.

It occurred to him then that he could be dying. If this was a sign of illness, it might be something rather severe.

He padded through the hall to his study and sat down at his computer, opened a browser and began searching. The cat came in and pawed his slippers. He was glad of another living thing. Apart from various articles on mental health, he found items on brain tumours and high blood pressure. He clicked the window closed. This was not sensible. He had papers to go over, work to complete. He would speak to Dr Turner tomorrow and not make any panicked guesses.

On the desk next to the computer was a framed picture of Akari sitting on a wall in Italy with a small beige lizard near her hand. She was holding up a lemon-coloured cocktail with a parasol in it. He wondered how to tell her. Whether she'd fret or try to minimise it. They'd met when he was twenty-two, and she was twenty-eight. He'd been travelling in Japan, working as an assistant in an English class. He'd been there three days when their paths had crossed in the school itself, where she was a music teacher for the clarinet and flute. Their first meeting was in the lunchroom – they'd sat down beside each other and not spoken for a while, being equally shy. She was originally from a village three hours from the school. Her father was a fisherman. They fell in love quickly. When he came home at the end of the year, he was engaged. His brother was disdainful. 'She saw you coming a mile off. A penniless Japanese spinster. Her parents will be dancing in the street.' Then at the wedding, Robert saw Akari and his brother talking together after all the dancing was done and most of the wine was gone and people were wilting at the tables in twos and threes. He left them to it, and they talked a long time, and after that, his brother was quietly respectful. Akari was both a worrier and a practical person. It was hard to know which way the news of his hallucinations would tip her.

The next day, he didn't call the doctor. Something had snagged in him, holding him back. In the evening, Akari was home, and all was calm. He didn't tell her; it all stayed locked inside his head. The day at court had been fairly average, except that at the moment when the jury delivered their guilty verdict for the woman accused of theft, she'd bellowed, 'You fuckers, you don't even care, I bet you all go out for lunch together after this. You're the worst, you didn't bother your arse at all.' It took a moment to realise that she was not talking to the jury but to himself and the lawyers, and the last comment was aimed at her defence solicitor, Simmons. The man was both arrogant and particularly handsome, which made him unsympathetic. But Robert felt a flash of pity as he saw Simmons looking down at his notes, his neck reddening.

The woman was half right though; her solicitor could have done a better job. He'd paused and drifted and spoken in a dull, husky voice. Maybe he was hungover or going down with the flu. 'You all go and enjoy your fucking pheasant stuffed with caviar,' the woman shouted. Robert was practised at not showing amusement. He told her to be quiet but did not hold her in contempt of court because she would be getting a custodial sentence anyway, given her previous record.

At home now, he left Akari to her electronic piano practise, and headed for his study to get through some journal articles. Everything was stable and peaceful, and he kept a window open because the evening was so warm, letting in the lulling sound of the wood pigeons, the scent of privet. Boyd didn't appear until after eleven when Robert was in the bath. He was thinking about nothing in particular, about a grandfather clock his dad had left him, how he had meant to get it ticking again, when he sensed the presence beside him. Instead of turning, he bowed his head over the olive-looking bathwater and saw the reflection of the figure lapping in the ripples. Every muscle tensed. He kept his head down – he could see the familiar clothing out of the corner of his eye. The grey of the suit coat, the white of the shirt, the bright sky blue of the tie. The figure said nothing but leant over him until he could feel hot breath on the hair at the back of his head. Could catch a faint sour scent. That was enough.

He let out a garbled scream and sat up. Boyd was gone. Seconds later, he could hear Akari rushing across the hall, calling. The bathwater rocked around him like a little ocean.

'What's happened, what's happened?'

'I'm fine,' he said.

'What on earth are you making that noise for?'

'I stubbed my toe on the tap. It's nothing.'

He sat in the water shivering and didn't climb out until the pads of his fingers were wrinkled in a way that reminded him of being a small boy – staying in the bath too long, playing with tin submarines.

By the time he got to the bedroom, Akari was reading with her glasses balanced halfway down her nose, the quilt covering her chest. They always slept naked because of something she'd read near the beginning of their marriage in a newspaper advice column. Akari was sixty-nine now to his sixty-three. Older women in films hid their bodies from men, but she never concealed anything from him.

He undressed, taking his shirt off first. He wondered about guilt. Did he feel any regret about the sentencing of this young man, more than any time before? The case was clear cut enough. Boyd had been convicted of *assault to injury* for an attack using a broken bottle. There had been previous convictions. The victim had been a former friend, and neither of them could give an account of why or how they'd fallen out. The attack had taken place in a pub in the daytime, both men were drunk and arguing. There were several witnesses who saw Boyd do it, including people who had no obvious connection to either of them. Boyd's fingerprints were on the broken bottle, and he'd had the victim's blood on his T-shirt and jeans. The forensics expert had shown that certain specifically shaped flecks of blood could only have come from being nearby at the moment of impact. Boyd's defence had been simply that he couldn't remember what happened that night, and he was completely unable to answer the questions put to him by the procurator fiscal, saying over and over, 'I don't know, I don't know, miss,' as if she was a primary school teacher and he'd lost the classroom hamster.

Boyd's mother had sat behind her son throughout the trial, her long face often disappearing into her cupped hands, but that was not uncommon, and Robert was not especially moved by it. When the guilty verdict came, it was the young man, not the mother, who cried. Again, not remarkable, and it stirred neither sympathy nor disdain in Robert.

It was true that the victim of the stabbing was no boy scout. At certain moments during cross-examination, he'd grinned like the fox who'd got the goose. When the defence put it to him that he didn't know who had stabbed him, that he'd been drunk, and had only named Boyd because he wanted compensation, he replied, 'It wasn't just me who saw, and course I want compensation, look at what happened to me.' He'd lifted his shirt to show the white zag of the stab wound for a second time. Cocky as he was, the incident must have been frightening and painful, and he'd needed three pints of blood. So often, Robert's cases involved these swaggering young men who wanted to believe they were something other than mortal creatures, that if they took a stabbing with the right attitude, they wouldn't bleed out and die in the way that a dog or a pig would.

He was quite sure that Boyd was guilty and that the sentence was fair. After the verdict, the defence had brought in a history of PTSD related to army service and stated the young man was attending therapy. But they so often were diagnosed with one thing or another, and plenty of people managed to have PTSD without stabbing anyone. Various other disadvantages in life were mentioned. The medic Lib McCullough sometimes complained that the courts mainly consisted of 'the upper-middle-classes judging the poor.' There was a pinch of truth in that, but Robert worked hard to take everything into account. By Boyd's record, he was asking for not a second chance but a fourth or fifth one.

So the sentencing had been no more difficult or easy than that of any other case.

. . .

The next morning as he listened to the opening questioning of the first witness for a sexual assault trial, he found himself thinking that the whole series of appearances were more like a haunting than what he thought of as hallucinations. He'd made up ghost stories as a boy, told them to his two chief friends whenever they got the chance to set up a fire behind the compost heap at his uncle's house. He'd been the best at telling them, half scaring himself as the three of them sat muffled in smoke.

In court, one ear attentive to the case, he wondered if Boyd might be dead. A suicide was just possible; he was in a high-risk category. Of course, this was a silly line of thought, and he was a man of reason. But the idea knocked up against something in his psyche.

During the first break, he took time to search for Boyd's name in any news stories online. Not a thing. The original case wasn't extreme enough to receive media coverage. He searched for prison deaths too. There was nothing local in the last week.

Arriving at court the following morning, he saw the defence solicitor who had worked on Boyd's case rushing through security, her coat sagging half off one shoulder, heavy bags hanging from the crook of her elbow. The coincidence of it struck him. He wondered if he could engineer a way to get hold of her. During lunch, he took a walk through the corridors of the courthouse, something he rarely did. After a good bit of wandering and avoiding people he didn't want to talk to, he turned a corner and caught sight of her, looking through notes outside court five. She was a slim, delicate seeming woman, perhaps in her early thirties. He stood nearby until she turned round and noticed him.

'Ah, hello,' he said as if surprised.

'Good afternoon.'

'Afternoon. Yes. Actually, useful to see you. I was wondering, how is that client of yours fairing? The one who got five years.'

'Oh. I saw him this morning to make sure he understands the appeal options. Not as bad as he could be. He'd been expecting a custodial sentence – I had prepped him for it, of course.' Her eyes on him. 'And you know how it is for some of these young men – prison is not exactly alien territory.' He nodded. She seemed pleased that he showed an interest. He had been a bit hard on her during the case, making remarks about her timing and organisation. She had a habit of looking at the floor when criticised, which had further irritated him in the moment.

'Was there something else you wanted to ask me?' she said.

'No, no. Just wondered. Thank you, good to know.'

The appearances had happened when he was alone, so that evening, he spent as much time with Akari as he could.

'Why are you being so clingy?' she said at last, stripping spring onions in the kitchen. 'Don't you have something better to do?' She was joking, but he took it as a cue to go away. He couldn't become afraid of being on his own, like a little boy. A part of him was almost looking forward to it in a tangled way, the rush of adrenaline. He could taste it coming like a frost in the air.

He seated himself in the study and searched on the computer, reading more about hallucinations. Severe psychiatric illnesses seemed to mostly start in youth and develop slowly over time. He looked for something else. He found references to Freud:

As with dreams, Freud believed that hallucinations were the product of the unconscious mind. Hallucinations with no phys-ical cause – or even sometimes hallucinations caused by a pathology – could represent hidden processes within the self.

So, guilt?

These processes might include unresolved sexual issues or neuroses.

Well of course, it was Freud. He brought to mind the image of the young man, arriving in the bedroom, the bathroom. Had there been something electric about it? Was this all to do with sex? Now that he thought about it, the shaved head aside, Boyd shared a resemblance with a male law student he'd had some drunken fumblings with forty-odd years ago. But he was never especially frightened by that. It was just a thing that had happened, he hadn't tried to delete the memory. 'If that's your game, I'm not impressed,' he said out loud. He thought about the young man as he appeared in the hallucinations. There seemed nothing specifically erotic about it. He shook off the idea. 'Bloody Freud.'

Could it just be the heat? He sat up and took his hands away from the keyboard. The unusual warmth and density of the air. In the last weeks, the sun had parched great yellow islands into the lawn. But the visitations happened in the evenings when the air was cooler. He'd certainly had nothing like heatstroke, which he knew all about from an ill-fated summer in Bavaria.

Just then, the brakes of a car screeched in the street, and he turned his head towards the window, the light filtering through the leaves of the tall beech tree in the front garden. It was nothing, the car restarted its engine and carried on. When he looked away from the window, he found that Boyd was standing in the room, over on the left-hand side of the desk, eyes hooded by tired lids. He was as solid and detailed as before.

'What are you for?' Robert said. 'What do you want me to know?'

He had the absurd notion that the thing was lonely. Or that it had come to him because it thought *he* was lonely. But it wasn't real, just a mistaken arrangement of firings somewhere in his visual cortex; it couldn't have thoughts or feelings of its own. He could see the hand more clearly now; the tattoo definitely showed a fishtail, the body disappearing into the sleeve. The face stayed the same, as blank as it had been most of the time in court, just that hint of fatigue about the eyes. The cat was settled on the spare bed behind the apparition, eyes half shut, pink paw pads flexing.

Robert got up. *Damn it to hell*, he would walk through the thing and see what happened.

But as he stood and took a step towards it, it was gone.

He sat heavily back down at the computer. He screwed his fists against his eyes. Not psychosis, not guilt, not a ghost, not repressed longings, not heatstroke. Before he left the house that day, he'd checked his blood pressure on his home monitor and found it perfectly average. That seemed to leave him with the most disturbing possibility. The brain tumour.

In the morning, he rose with Akari. Saturday and rest had come.

'I want to have breakfast outside,' he said.

'It's a bit of a bother.'

'I want to.'

He led her out and brought all the cutlery and plates to the small, metal garden table. They sat opposite each other, the cat dancing round their ankles in the hope of scraps. He thought of various ways to say it, but in the end, it came out as: 'I've been seeing a man who isn't there.'

Akari stopped eating and reached her fingers toward his. 'How so?'

'I've seen him in the conservatory, in the bedroom, in the bathroom, in the study. Over the last few days. Someone from court. But he's not really there. He just vanishes.' Akari's eyes were widening. Without meaning to, he added, 'Could it be... could he be some kind of spirit?'

'No,' Akari said. 'No. I think you're not well in some way.' She raised a hand, and for a moment, he thought she was going to place it against his forehead as you would do with a feverish child, but instead, she brushed aside a leaf that had fallen onto his sleeve.

'I suppose it might be a brain problem. A tumour maybe,' he said.

'It could be anything. Don't assume the worst,' she said. But then she began to cry. Not sobbing or dabbing at her eyes, just letting tears spill over. He had not expected that. She was not someone who cried.

'We've been a long way, you and I, haven't we?' he said. 'My mind can't make sense of one of us left alone.'

'I know, I know.'

'I've made a private appointment for Monday, to get a scan.'

'Well, that'll tell us something. We don't know anything yet. We can't guess. We're here now...' She looked around them as if checking that the garden was still there. Starlings clustered beside them on the birdfeeder. 'Let's try to enjoy the sun.' She dipped her head to acknowledge his effort with the table, 'It was a good idea to have breakfast outside, let's not spoil it.' She put her spoon into her yogurt and honey, eyes wavering with tears.

'Yes, only sensible thing. We can't influence the outcome by fretting. We just don't know yet,' he said, and he poured out coffee for them both. Akari began eating, sweet little mouthfuls in the hot sun, though the tears kept rolling down her face.

He saw nothing on the Saturday, or during the day on the Sunday. When the night came, he couldn't sleep. There was no cool part of the mattress left. After Akari drifted off, he found himself going over an old case, through broken bits of half-remembered argument. It was one of his earliest cases as a defence solicitor, a woman he could not prevent from being convicted of arson. She was accused of setting a fire in her own flat, which had burned through to her neighbour's. No one was injured, except the accused herself, whose hands were badly burned. She claimed it was accidental, but the jury didn't believe her. The remains of firelighters were found in her kitchen. He'd wondered if she was mentally unwell in some way, but there had been no such finding. She was middle-aged, seeming old to him then but probably much younger than he was now. A heavyset woman with soft rolling flesh under her arms, she wore a small silver cross. He'd had an overwhelming urge to protect her, a pull he never felt again to the same extent with any client. When the verdict had come, she didn't look at him, only at her own bandaged hands gripping the edge of the dock. Lying in bed now, he ran over the phrasing he could have used, the different tilts he could have given the evidence, whether it would have made any difference. This struggling with old cases or judgements often happened in the boggy ground before sleep. Something about lying still in the dark. He sat up in the hot quilt and let the thoughts of the case drain out of him. No sense in reliving these things. He pinched the bridge of his nose and got out of bed. The case sifted away.

He tiptoed to the bedroom window. Akari was still sleeping, making a noise that was not quite snoring. It needled him the way she had cried. At least she slept soundly now. When they had first got together, it had been Akari who had trouble sleeping. She had often risen in the night and gone to the fridge and made elaborate snacks for herself, piling things onto rye crackers. Or he'd find her nibbling a bitter dark chocolate bar in the living room, fumbling with the static on the radio. He hadn't known how to ask if she was homesick; maybe he'd been afraid she would say yes and want to leave him. When he asked her years later, she said, 'It was more that I was always alert. Like I had to take everything in, all the new things.'

She'd felt the cold in those days too. Their first winter in the flat up in Aberdeen, she'd piled blankets onto their bed so it became like an animal's burrow. She always used two hot water bottles then, one at her feet, one at her midriff. Beside her, he would be soaked in sweat. They'd had sex most nights in those early years, curling against each other afterwards, so that he'd thought a baby might simply happen any day, that he'd come home from court, and she'd announce it in the kitchen. When that moment never transpired, there was a dim sense that they were both relieved, that they liked their life as it was, and without much discussion, they took no medical steps.

A sea-change occurred in the middle of their marriage so that Akari became the one who slept easily, and also the one who felt the heat, frequently tutting and turning down the thermostat. With his appointment to the judiciary, his sleep had become broken. 'You stand over other people's lives,' she'd said by way of explanation. He'd protested, he had rules to follow, and he'd always had to take his job seriously. But she shook her head and said it again. Other people's lives, not in his hands, but underneath him, at his feet.

Opening the curtains to look out the dark window, he doubted he'd get to sleep now. If this thing didn't end, he might have to stop working. What would he be then if he was no longer a judge? He'd be only a pair of eyes looking out on the world. In the garden, the light was coming, and he could begin to see shapes and dull colours. A white haze that seemed out of place. He narrowed his eyes. He couldn't believe it. A man in a white shirt was on the lawn. At first, he thought it was a would-be burglar. Then he realised, of course, it was Boyd, standing there by the garden shed. The apparition was breaking the rules, it seemed, by appearing outside, and without his suit coat. The figure moved onto the flagstone path and stood still, looking straight ahead. At the same time, in the bedroom, something touched the small of his back. He jumped. It was Akari. She had got out of bed without his hearing.

'What are you looking at?'

'It's him.'

'Where?'

'On the path by the shed.' The figure was still there, despite Akari standing beside him. That seemed another rule broken. Robert pointed. 'You can't see him, of course?'

'No. I wish I could.'

'You don't want to see him.' He became afraid that Boyd would look up at the window and there would be something wrong with his face. It would be melted into a skull or have a piece missing, the nose or an eye. But the figure kept staring straight ahead.

'I want to see what you see,' Akari said. She had put on her thin dressing gown. Her shoulder brushed his. She was trembling beside him, but her voice was calming. 'What does he look like?'

'From here, just an ordinary young man with a shaved head. He's not looking at us. He's got a white shirt on. He's not wearing his jacket or tie like he usually does.'

'He's changed?'

'A little bit.'

'That might be good.'

'Or bad.'

'I hope he finds peace.'

He turned to her, confused in the dark. 'He's not dead, he's not a ghost.'

She shook his shoulder. 'I know that. But I hope it anyway. The real man. Wherever he is.'

'He's in prison.'

'Well.'

'We'll get through this,' he said. 'We'll get the verdict tomorrow, or at least more information to go by.'

'Later today, I guess.'

'Later today. Whatever it is, we'll fight it.' He blinked hard, and the figure vanished. Akari's eyes wandered over the pane of glass.

'Is he gone now?' she said as if she sensed his body easing.

'Yes, he's gone.'

'Good. Stay away, please, sir.' He looked at her to see if she was joking, but she didn't smile. In the half-light below them, the cat stalked across the parched grass. The two of them continued to stand side by side at the window. Together they watched the new day form, out of the deep blue shadows of the garden.

The Dog Husband

Jean first laid eyes on the animal at the school sports day. She was watching the children race, their legs hidden in empty potato sacks, when she spotted Moira on the other side of the ribbon barrier. Standing in her buckled boots with a collie on a lead at her heel. Moira had not owned a dog before. This one was a nimble looking thing with a harlequin-patched face. The children bounced over the finish line, a troupe of wallabies. Jean's boy came third, glum with concentration. She cheered, clapped, made her way round.

The dog noticed her before Moira did, its nose pointing her out. Moira was often standing alone. People were afraid of saying the wrong thing to a widow. Even the word was off-putting, with its connotations of spider's venom.

'Who's this then?' Jean said.

'Got him from the mainland.' Moira reached down and scuffled the dog's head. The tiny tan markings that looked like eyebrows shifted upwards.

'Not a bad idea to get an adult dog. Puppies can be such a hassle.' But she thought it was odd, the dog the kind that should be on a farm nipping at the heels of black-faced sheep. 'Do the boys like him?'

'It's amazing really. They lollop around together. They spent the whole afternoon in the fields yesterday.'

'That's lucky. They might not have taken to each other.' Maybe Moira got the dog because she'd been afraid in the house alone. Together they watched the egg and spoon race, the ladles and the multi-coloured plasticine eggs which hit the ground without breaking. One of Moira's boys came first. She bobbed onto her toes. Jean elbowed her. 'There you go!'

Moira settled, took a small breath like a sigh and said, 'Listen, I'll tell you a secret.' She ran the dog's right ear through her fingers. She was smiling, like it was something mischievous. In front of them, the kids moved on to the three-legged race, roping themselves together at the ankles or knees.

'Yeah, go on?'

Moira's smile drew in, and Jean sensed she was about to be told something she didn't want to hear.

'Things are going to get better now,' said Moira.

'How'd you mean?'

'It's the dog.'

'In what way?'

Moira paused, her lips twitched. Around the playing field, little things kept catching the light. A jug of water, a metal clip on a teacher's I.D. laminate, the brass tag on the dog's collar. Glints like minnows in a river.

'The thing is, listen. The dog is Richard.' She held up her hand to stop Jean from cutting in. 'Och, this is going to sound mad. But the dog is Richard somehow. He's come back to me.'

Jean brought her fingers up to the neck of her jumper and pulled the fabric away an inch from her skin. 'Oh no, Moira. Oh no, no, no.'

. . .

Richard had died on the mainland, a heart attack at the fuel station, and they'd had those resuscitation machines there, the ones they'd fundraised for, and it hadn't made any difference. Moira had been working in the primary school office on the island when it happened. By the time the hospital phoned her, he was already gone. Jean had heard the news the following morning as she set out to buy the papers, and it had made her feel sick and small and tight. The thing that had comforted her, though she would never say it out loud, was the thought that Richard had been a smoker. No one in Jean's family smoked. Also, she'd seen him tip a long line of salt onto a fried egg, pouring it from the porcelain salt cellar like a white ribbon.

The Sunday after the games day, Jean was at her friend Rhona's house, making apple cakes for the bake sale. Standing in the gleaming kitchen where everything seemed over large, unsettlingly clean.

'A funny thing yesterday. I was talking to Moira and she's gone and got a collie dog,' Jean said.

'What did she do that for? She barely exercises, a collie will walk her off her feet.'

'Well, that's it. And there's another strange thing.'

'Like what?'

'Well.' Jean was, all at once, embarrassed on Moira's behalf.

'Yeah?'

'She told me... she said to me... she thinks it's her husband.'

'What do you mean?'

'She thinks the dog's Richard. Back from the dead. I don't know. Reincarnated or something.'

Rhona gave a short laugh. 'She has got her sense of humour back then.'

'No, no, she wasn't joking.'

'Of course she was,' Rhona said. 'She's not daft. Where'd she get the dog from?'

'On the mainland somewhere. I don't know. But it didn't seem like she was joking.'

'Love, she was having you on.' Rhona stared at her with hard blue eyes.

'Well, I mean, I knew she was joking a bit, but it seemed odd. Sort of sick in a way. You know, with her kids around, to joke about their dad...'

'Jean, come on. Are you sure you knew she was joking?'

Sometimes Jean didn't like Rhona, and she was her main friend on the island. Jean had made the move three years ago, herself and her son and her boyfriend. Sometimes the island seemed tiny as a mussel shell.

'Yes, I did know. I'm just worried about her.'

'Why would you worry? Were the boys right next to her?'

'No, they were out racing.'

'Well, there you go,' Rhona said. 'She was pulling your leg. You are daft sometimes.'

Rhona took the apple sauce from her and started spooning it into the bowl with the other ingredients. Jean was over-heated, with the oven warming up. Before the island, she'd never thought of herself as a person who'd make cakes for a bake sale. Her clothes were smothering her, drops of sweat galloping down her sides. She moved to open the kitchen window, to let in a shaft of island air.

The day of the bake sale, it was raining steady and straight, and so they took shelter in the town hall, and people came in ones and twos, making ghostly mud prints on the hall floor.

An hour or so in, Moira arrived. She had her dog with her, its claws clicking on the waxed floorboards. Jean was on her own at the stall.

'These look gorgeous. Did you make them?' Moira leaned across the table, the dog standing like a small sentry at her feet.

'Me and Rhona. They've got apple sauce in. Actually, they're pretty much mainly apple sauce. They might be a bit soggy.'

'I'll take four. One for each of us.'

Jean slid the cakes into a brown paper bag. Four must mean one for the dog. Without looking up, she said, 'Listen, I'm sorry about last week – I didn't get that you were joking.'

'About what?'

'About the dog.'

'About the dog being Richard?'

'Yes.'

'I wasn't.' Moira took the bag of cakes from her, folding over the top. 'No, I wasn't joking.'

'Oh.' Warmth began to spread across her neck. It would form that pink fan shape she got sometimes.

'I sort of wish I hadn't said anything now because it must sound nuts, but there you go. How much is that then?'

'Two pounds,' Jean said.

Moira handed over a couple of coins. Jean put the money in the ice cream tub they were using as a change-box. All further words were gone from her. She could smell the dampness of the dog now, its pinkish-blue tongue lolling. A man came in behind Moira, a tourist wearing a penguin poncho, and the collie turned to look.

'Well, I'll let you serve someone else. See you around,' Moira said.

'See you.'

Jean stepped backwards as Moira turned away. The thought came into her head: *it is not safe to be near madness.*

Walking on the strip of sand they called the otter beach on the far side of the island, Jean told her boyfriend about Moira and the dog.

'What are we going to do?'

'Why would we need to do anything?' he said.

'She's not well. She's, you know, slipped her moorings.'

'She's grieving.'

'It's been a year,' Jean said. 'And that's not the point, what she said is just mad. It would be crazy if she was going around saying it the day after he died.'

'She's not hurting anyone by believing that. Maybe it's a comfort?'

'To think that her husband is a fucking dog?'

'Well, perhaps,' he said, slowing his step.

'What are we going to do, though?'

'Why would we need to do anything?'

She wanted to say, *because she might be dangerous.* She knew in the core of her heart it was not true; Moira was about as dangerous as an old wool hat. But she wanted to say it. And to add, *because the dead are gone.*

The dead are gone in the same way that the children in the Pied Piper of Hamlin were gone, swallowed up by the mountainside, with the stones sealed behind them. Her own sister died thirty years ago, and she had known since the day she was given the news in the teachers' lunchroom that her big sister was no longer part of the world. They broke it to her in that pokey, crumbling staffroom, and she'd stood and listened, watching her distorted reflection in the kettle, and she'd known. You couldn't just rehome a ragged mutt and start proclaiming that the dead had risen. If things like that were possible, she would have done it herself. She wanted to say all of that to her boyfriend as they walked on the beach, but instead she moved ahead and kept her eyes on the squirrelling line of the horizon.

The ferry bobbed in the smoke-coloured waters. Jean was going to town to buy an oil heater. Moira was on the boat somewhere; Jean had seen her walk across the ramp with her shopping trolley. The loping dog by her side. Right now, she must be fixing the trolley in place in the luggage compartment. Jean waited.

Soon she heard the clung, clung sound of someone climbing the metal steps to the seating area. There Moira was, stepping through the door with her purse in one hand and the dog's lead in the other as if everything was normal and she was not mad.

'Hi there,' Jean said.

'Hello.' The dog followed Moira with its nose to the back of her knees.

'How are you?'

'Good, good.' Moira sat down, and the dog hunkered edgily at her feet. 'Good,' she added, as if Jean had asked again, and then, 'Another thing happened about the dog. I know you don't believe me, but it was uncanny.'

'What happened?'

'I came back yesterday and he was holding Richard's shoe in his mouth. He was waiting for me as I came in through the door.'

Jean looked ahead to the circle of window. 'But, Moira, dogs like shoes, don't they? Dogs like to chew shoes.'

'Of all the things he could have chosen. I opened the door, and that's the first thing I saw. It'd been tucked away in a cupboard somewhere, and he'd gone and found it and brought it to me. As if he was saying, *here I am.*'

Jean spoke very clearly. 'But that doesn't mean anything. Dogs gnaw shoes, they like the way they smell.'

Moira sat facing forwards too, not looking at her. 'Uncanny, that's the word.'

'Sorry. I don't want to hear this. I can't listen. I'm going to sit outside.' She stood up. Moira's eyes were on her now, unsurprised, as if she'd known she'd push her out. Jean walked towards the door. She thought of her son's science homework, the matching poles of two magnets repelling each other by invisible means. Words came into her head: *You lunatic bitch.* The words sat there on the spongey centre of her tongue. She was not a mean person, but how could anyone be so wilfully crazy? She held her tongue between her front teeth, didn't bite it but gripped it. Even when she'd got out of sight, she could feel Moira's gaze on the back of her skull.

She took a seat on the outer viewing deck. The air was cold against her face and neck and hands. Waves extended from the boat like white arrows pointing back to shore. To the small, tight space of the island. The shell of it. When they arrived on the pier at the other side, she waited for Moira and the dog to leave first.

Someone had placed a dead gull on the grass, rotting, outside Jean's house. She stood staring in the morning light. The feathers were stained with the butterscotch colour of decay. When her boyfriend came into the living room with his coffee, she pointed it out to him.

'What if Moira left it there?' she said.

'Moira? Bloody hell. Of course not, it was a fox or something. Jesus. Why on earth would she do that?'

'There aren't foxes on the island, you know that. And I was rude to her, wasn't I? I didn't mean to be, but I just couldn't listen to any more of that crap.'

Was it Moira? There was no reason to think so, really. But the dirty feathers gave her an uneasy feeling. The morning sun created long, westerly shadows. A striped cat sat licking its paw on the path, ignoring the gull. Why wasn't it eating the dead bird? A normal cat would go and investigate. Everything was turning on the island, an oddness creeping in all over.

Knowing she shouldn't, she added, 'I mean, where does the dog sleep?'

'Why does that matter?'

'You know. Where does the dog sleep?'

'What are you saying?'

'If she thinks it's her husband, does it sleep in her bedroom?'

Her boyfriend's lips parted, closed, then parted again. 'If you're saying what I think you're saying, you've got a twisted mind.'

'I'm just putting two and two together.'

'Jean, she's not mental,' he said.

'But that's just the problem – she *is* mental.'

He balanced his coffee on the windowsill and squinted at the bird. 'Honestly...'

They stood together for a while, then she said, 'You might have made me a cup.'

'Please is a nice word.' He turned and left the room, possibly to get another coffee, possibly not. She stayed looking at the gull. There were footprints on the road, out in the dirt, but that didn't prove anything. The cat carried on washing delicately.

Jean walked round to pick her son up from Rhona's house. She'd told Rhona about it all on the phone. Even the seagull. She wished she hadn't said that last part now because it sounded silly, but it had to spill out. The evening was cool, a slight smoky taste to the air, the days getting fractionally shorter. She stood outside Rhona's door, shivering.

'What are we going to do? I know it's nasty, but I'm not sure I want my son spending time with her boys,' Jean said. The moon hung beside them to the east in the blue evening sky, a thumbprint of talc.

'She'll straighten her head out in a year or two. Grief makes people see the world in a funny way.'

'But she's going crazy.'

'Bereavement makes people a bit unhinged.'

Jean wanted to say, *no, no, no*. She had missed her sister, her grandparents, her mother, from the first moment after each death was revealed, but that hadn't given her the right to go a bit unhinged. She had stayed fully attached to life, entirely hinged.

Her son appeared at the door, a flank of hair smoothed across his eyes.

'Take care now. I don't think you should mention about the seagull to anyone else,' said Rhona.

Jean gave a minimal nod. She and her son walked home together, the boy bashing at the hedgerows with a stick. All the way, they could hear the sound of the waves lapping. With each step, she became more and more sure about the gull. The island seemed so cramped sometimes. The size of a cowrie.

The dead are dead, she wanted to shout, so that her voice boomed from one shore to the other.

The next morning the seagull was gone, but there was a dead rabbit lying on the lawn about two metres from where the gull had been. She stood looking at the torn rabbit for a long time, wondering who to tell. In the end, she decided she would tell no one. Moira could bloody well have it back.

At ten past nine, when Moira would be at work and the boys at school, she took the rabbit up to Moira's house, wrapped in a plastic bin liner. If it hadn't really been Moira, no one would see anyway, and at least she wouldn't have to keep looking at the rabbit out the window, the red gash of its stomach.

She reached Moira's front garden. She realised she still thought of the house as Moira and Richard's place. She put the rabbit into the hedge as if she was placing a baby down in a cradle.

Just as it was settled, she caught sight of the blur of a face at the porch window. Moira's youngest son was looking out at her. She stood still.

The boy opened the door and planted one foot on the step. He had big, brown doe eyes like Richard. 'What are you doing?' he said. He wiped at his nose with his sleeve. His russet hair standing on end. He was in his pyjamas. An orphan. Or half an orphan.

'Nothing, nothing. You should be at school.'

'I'm not well.' He looked at her as if to say, *you shouldn't be in my garden putting a dead rabbit in my hedge.* If he was off sick, Moira would be at home too. Moira was possibly watching her from a window right now.

'Well, I hope you're much better soon,' she said. He carried on looking at her and the collie dog appeared behind him in the porch and peered at her too. Also, with deep brown eyes.

Because she could not now own up to placing the rabbit by taking it back, she did the only thing she could think of and walked away with the boy and the dog watching her go, seeing her off.

She waited for another dead animal to appear, but there wasn't one. Next Saturday at the co-op, whilst getting the dinner things, she thought she heard Lewis on the till lean over and say to Mr Martin, '...put a dead rabbit in her hedge.'

She wanted to run over and say, *no, no, it's her who's mad.* There was dead-rabbit-in-a-hedge eccentricity, and there was collie-dog-as-the-father-of-your-children insanity. But she might have misheard. Perhaps he said, *put the rarebit with some veg,* or *better grab it off the window ledge.* She knew she was hearing what she was afraid they'd say.

She paid for her pasta and mince and tomato sauce and onions. As she left with her shopping bag, she heard Lewis utter the phrase, *slipped her moorings,* to the customer behind her. Her own words, which she had said about Moira. But surely this too was not what Lewis had really said.

That night she found herself writing Moira a note. Her son was sprawled on the carpet in front of the television, doing his homework in the advert breaks. *Dear Moira,* she wrote, *I'm crazy too, let's be friends again.*

'When Vikings die, they put them in a boat and set them on fire,' her son said, turning, the glow from the screen highlighting his nose and cheekbones.

'That's interesting.' She had a vague feeling this was a myth, but she didn't want to disappoint him.

'They put everything they owned in the boat so they can take it to the afterlife.'

'Oh, cool.' She didn't want to think of funerals and burnings and afterlives. She looked at the note she'd written. She couldn't imagine handing it over, how that could come about. What would Moira be thinking of her if she did see her place the rabbit? She felt as if her insides were coated with tar. When her son next looked down at his book, she ripped up the note and slipped the pieces into the crevice behind the sofa cushion.

Her boyfriend was driving. They were going to pick up their son from another school friend's house, where he'd been playing with his bucket of plastic robot cars.

They passed Moira's house on the way out. Moira and Richard's. The layout of the island was as familiar to her as the inside of her wallet. Once the house was behind them and they were driving between the high hedgerows of the fields beyond, her boyfriend glanced at her, raising an eyebrow. 'That reminds me, I said he could go on a camping trip with Moira and her boys.'

'Why would you say that?'

'Well, why not?'

'Because you should ask me first? I might not want him to go.'

'But they play together all the time at school,' he said.

'But it's different, a camping trip. What if she takes the dog?'

'She probably will. What does that matter? He's not scared of dogs.'

'You know why it matters. You can't just make decisions like that without asking me.'

'How does that even count as a decision? It's nothing.' His voice was raising, his hands fluttering off the wheel. She could not raise her voice; he would accuse her of shouting.

'If you thought it was nothing, you wouldn't have given me that bloody sheepish look. What if she tells him the dog's Richard? What if her sons call it dad?'

Her boyfriend turned to her saying, 'For God's sake,' and at the same time, she could see through the windscreen, a blur of blue and red, something he had not seen. She was unable to make sense of it and also understood absolutely. A boy dashing out from a gap in the hedgerow towards the field gate on the other side. Even in the whirl of it, she recognised Moira's oldest kid. She tried to say something in words, but instead she made a bark of panic. Her boyfriend returned his eyes to the road and also let out an animal sound. He swerved the car left of the boy, hit the brakes, but there was still a horrible thunk, a judder, and then they were stopping, throwing open the doors.

They ran around the front of the car. On the ground by the wheel was the collie dog. The boy stood at the gate, his mouth clamped shut, his hands reaching behind him to grip the bars. The tall grass of the field beyond danced in the breeze. Even though they could see blood, even though a tang of iron was in the air and the dog was lying flat out, its tail was wagging, beating the ground. Jean knew that dogs wagged their tails sometimes as a sign of extreme stress. Yet, in that jangling moment, as the dog rose its head and looked over its shoulder at her, it seemed to be saying, *I'm glad I took the hit, I took it for my boy.*

.   .   .

The autumn deepened, hardened, and finally crystallised into winter, the days becoming small and cold like chips of ice. Moira and her sons had gone away to the mainland abruptly one weekend two months back. Ostensibly to visit with relatives, there were rumours about her having a stay in one of the big psychiatric hospitals in Edinburgh or Glasgow. People wondered in gentle tones if she and the kids would ever return.

But on a Saturday morning at the end of January, when Jean was sitting alone in the porch drinking a cup of tea, there Moira was out in the winter barley field beyond her house. Walking with the dog beside her in the pale light. Jean thought someone might have decided to take the animal away from her. But no, there was Moira returned, strolling out with her slinking, trotting, dog-husband, who kept a decent pace on his three good legs. It had been impossible to tell her that the dog had not deliberately saved the boy. The reality was they would have hit nothing, just rumbled along the verge, if the dog hadn't been there. They had paid for the veterinary bills. Instead of being angry afterwards, Moira had grabbed their hands, saying, *I know for certain now*.

Watching her from the window, Jean had an urge to open the front door and shout, *you lunatic, you lunatic*, but she smothered it, only mouthed the words and giggled. She willed Moira to look round and see her, but instead, she kept on facing away, walking her dog. Wearing her red winter coat and her biker boots, her curly hair blowing in the breeze, she kept on striding out with the collie, which she very probably still thought was the father of her kids. A woman looking so normal, looking so sane.

And also, somehow, giving the air of a person who had a lot of open ground around her, like she was walking on the mainland. As if the country stretched on forever round about her, and she was not on an island at all.

The King of France Wears a Hat

The palace had no odour. She was the last to walk in. Outside, the courtyard smelt of honey and warm bark. Inside the wide corridor, there was only cool, scentless air. Kay touched the doorframe, the walls, the thick dimpled glass of the window, a red strip on her wrist as her ticket. She trailed behind the others, hoping a proper gap would form.

Through the high door and on to the announcing hall, the pupils stopped in a huddle while she hung back. The teacher explained this was where the dignitaries and penniless relatives would wait before they saw the king. 'Imagine how you would feel sitting here, under all these images of power.' The painting above her head showed a man resting his foot on a stag's neck. The king had been assassinated one hundred and fourteen years ago, the teacher said. 'Later, you will see the carriage with the bullet holes in it.'

Through the next door, they trooped into the reception room, dotted with chairs of all types and sizes, the walls covered in story-telling tapestries. She kept herself behind, slowing her paces as they slowed. If she could hold the gap, they wouldn't remember she was there, and they would think nothing of her. 'The present King of France wears a hat,' the teacher said and looked at the pupils in that irritating way that meant she was actively teaching them. 'Is that statement true or false?'

'But this is nae France,' said one of the boys.

'That's not the point.'

'The statement is false,' said one of the girls.

'Why?'

'It's false, the King of France doesn't wear a hat because there is no King of France.'

'Alright, OK,' said the teacher. 'But if the statement is false – the present King of France wears a hat – false – then doesn't that mean there exists a King of France who doesn't wear a hat?'

'Aye, it does, boom, you're wrong,' the boy said, pointing at the girl, who took hold of his finger and pretended to twist it off.

'True then.'

'So there's a King of France who wears a hat?' the teacher said.

Kay tuned out of the conversation. Nearest to her was a chair covered in red fuzz, its legs looked like they were moulded from gold. She wanted to reach out to stroke the fuzz, but a small card saying *do not touch* in three languages sat on the cushion. On the far wall, three men with turbans gazed at her out of a swirling silver frame. She wondered who they were. They must be long dead. What would they think if they could see her through their painted eyes? She had a brightness in her, which other people couldn't see, and a dullness, which they could. Maybe these men would think of her in the same way the other pupils did: *here is a dull girl looking at us dimly*. In the early years of high school, other children had pushed her down the stairs and called her *k for cunt*. In this last year, everything had shifted, the pupils sat around the common room and talked about novels and philosophy and what was bad taste. Any cruelty was small, hidden, like the pips in satsumas. Sometimes the other kids called her *Magnolia*, after the paint colour, because, they said, she was bland. *You don't mind us calling you that, it's a joke.*

The group moved through to a room with one wall made entirely of glass. The air in the room was gently heated by the sun. The other walls were covered in tiles, creating soft echoes and giving off the feeling of a swimming pool. Ferns in terracotta pots hung from the ceiling. On three heavy chests of drawers, there perched three complicated bird cages with passageways and chambers, like miniature palaces. There were no birds in the cages. A candy-smelling breeze blew through an open pane in the glass wall. While the teacher talked, Kay imagined the birds that would have been. Clever and small, they were turquoise and pink and purple, like no birds she'd seen in life.

The pupils were in their last year of school. Soon they would leave. It was not considered a good school. The eight of them on the trip made up half of the kids in the final year. Sixteen had stayed; all their other contemporaries had gone straight into work or signed on. The pupils on the trip were considered the smart ones, the ones who might go to university. Even so, Kay did not fit with them. She regarded each of them with the wariness of a fox watching a dog. She was hungry with a teenager's desire, but she cast it elsewhere, not onto their bodies but at figures in films, in books, on the television. This strange last year where they were about to escape into the promised better lives, she wanted the world to split open and offer her something. (She'll dream of this year for decades to come, long into adulthood when her life will be something else. She'll dream of being back in this year, waiting to escape, wondering why it's not over yet. She will dream of this trip, in particular, of the rooms in the palace).

The teacher moved through the door marked exit and on into the corridor. The other pupils followed, Kay stayed. A breach opened up again. Kay let the gap stretch like chewed gum. She ran her tongue around her mouth, thought how her teeth were like a royal family; the two at the front were the king and queen with the dukes and duchesses round the sides, the servants were the molars at the back. When the last person disappeared into the hall, she was alone in the glass-walled room with the ferns and the birdcages. There was a different way of breathing when she was on her own, her lungs became wide spaces. Her brightness was stronger when there was no one to not see it.

One chair in the tiled room stood out because it was plain and grey and modern looking. It had no card on it. She stepped over to it and lowered herself slowly in case an alarm would go off. Nothing happened. The gap was stretching, stretching, stretching. The teacher's voice became fainter, the pupils' replies too. All their voices like tinkling bells.

The moment she could no longer hear them, she saw something moving in the cage closest to her. A tiny brown bird. She watched it, moving, bobbing, hopping. Why hadn't she noticed it before? A wee plain thing like a mouse with wings, unlike the birds she'd imagined.

Another movement. For a second, it seemed a black void was forming inside the cage. But no, just a door opening on the other side of the room; she could see it through the bars.

The door swung right back, and a man walked into the room. He was wearing a kind of costume, a white military-style jacket with a row of brass buttons on the front, badges on the pockets, patches on the shoulders. He walked over to an embroidered green couch and frowned for a fraction of a second as if he was looking at the card that said not to sit down. Then he sat as if it was not there. A newspaper was folded beside him. He picked it up and started to read. He had a moustache, thin and auburn coloured like a baby weasel.

After a time, he reached out to the low table in front of him and rang a brass handbell. A man dressed in another kind of uniform, blue like a dress-up version of a soldier's coat, came in and spoke to him in a language Kay didn't understand. The man in the blue coat gave a sharp nod and stepped out again. The man in the white jacket carried on reading. Kay breathed quietly into the room. In the birdcage, the tiny brown bird was hopping and fluttering.

A few minutes passed, the man in blue returned and put down a silver tray containing two small, flower-patterned cups and a tall brass pot. He poured a dark brown liquid into the cups; only a small drop into the first, the second one filled to the top. He lifted the first cup, drained it, nodded once, and backed out of the room. The man in white picked up the full cup. He took sips between curls of steam. Not coffee; she could smell it now, the sweet unfolding of chocolate. Turning her head slightly, she could see out through the glass wall, down across the city. The view might have been an old painting, greens and browns hazed by the heat. A more peaceful and still city than it had seemed going through the streets on the clanging tram.

The two men in their costumes, it was like one of her daydreams where she would slip into the past, walk around a street corner and find the cars had become horses and carriages. But it was not the past beyond the glass wall, she could see the cars and coaches and mopeds parked along the edge of the hill, their windscreens reflecting the sun. The men must be actors. They must be trained not to interact with visitors.

She turned back to look at the man in the white uniform, and as she did, he lowered his cup and looked round at her or past her. He put the cup down on the tray with a chink and rose slowly, his brow tensing. He began walking towards where she sat. It was as if he was looking at a mark on the chair itself. One step, then another. She could see the mottled pink colour of his cheeks. His complexion was pale for some-one of this country. How old he was, she could not have said. He came close, within half a metre. Another step, and he leant forward. The fingers on his left hand spread out, circled by heavy rings. She had never seen a man wear rings with gem-stones in them. She wondered if he was going to touch her, her face or her chest. She could get the scent of him. Sweat un-der perfume and his breathe smelt of chocolate, and beneath that, there was mackerel, just a hint of it. They must be ac-tors. She thought this, and another clear thought followed. He could not see her, and if that was to change, if he was to see her now, she would die.

His hand kept moving forward though he still was not looking at her. His fingers brushed a curl of her hair at the side of her forehead. She felt the tickle of it. She'd had a sense if he touched her, his hand would go right through her, but instead she felt the connection. His hand drew back. He straightened up, puffed air out of his lips. She tilted her head to see his face. He looked puzzled, as if he could not place what he had touched. She thought he was going to move away, but he reached his other hand forward. The splayed fingers of his right hand moved towards her chest. Tiny, incremental move-ments. Time seemed to slow to a sizzle. The pads of his fin-gers reached the triangle of skin where the opening of her shirt buttons stopped, formed a kind of star above her breast-bone and pressed there. Electric, then solid. She felt his hand could push on through her, her chest would become like wet clay. Again the thought, *he cannot see me, if he does I will die.* He stood still, breathing, and she inhaled his breath. He was still looking over her head. She could feel her own heartbeat against his fingertips.

Gazing straight at his midriff, she reached up to touch his hand, to feel whether it was warm or cold, but as she did so, he snatched his arm away. He turned and stepped back towards the couch. He picked the paper up and reversed the fold in it, sat down and began to read again. Kay stayed motionless, breathing deep.

After a time, minutes maybe, the blue-jacketed man came in again. The two men had a conversation in their language, the man in the white uniform making hard gestures with his hands. Finally, the man in white stood up, replaced the paper, and walked out of the room, his stride determined. The man in blue followed, quick steps. The door behind the birdcage closed. The cup of chocolate was still on the table, and the newspaper lay folded on the couch. The bird in the cage flitted from perch to perch, a brown leaf blown in the wind.

Kay stood noiselessly. She walked over towards the tray, placing her feet as if she were stepping across gravel and had to make as little noise as possible. When she reached the couch, she leant forward and dipped a finger into the chocolate and brought it to her lips. The liquid was warm, the taste gently spiced. She turned and walked out of the room through the door with the exit sign above. Small sparks seemed to spread out over her body.

Along the corridor, she saw no staff or tourists. And then there was noise, babbling voices, as if a switch had been flicked. She turned a corner and saw the grey and black clothes of her school group. She joined them down a flight of white marble steps. They were gathered in a huge basement space with nothing but an empty carriage and a plaque on the wall. The carriage rested, enormous and black, like something waiting to go to a funeral. She couldn't see where the bullet holes were. The group was still talking about the King of France.

'It's a problem in logic,' the teacher said. 'Uncertain truth value. Not everything is either true or false.'

'So what?' said the boy who had answered earlier.

'I still think it's just false. People make problems where there aren't any,' said the girl who'd spoken before. Kay slotted into her space at the back and followed the group. The sparks continued to spread over her, down her arms and legs. She ran her tongue along her teeth; an enamel royal family.

The school group passed through another set of rooms crowded with dark paintings and faded furniture, and out again into the courtyard that smelt of warm bark. The sparks spread to Kay's neck, to her lips. Perhaps she would disappear with a spatter of sparks like a lit firework. On the cobblestones, starlings bickered, above her the sky was cloudless blue. Through the great archway, the city stretched on and down in pastel greens and gold, the mopeds glinting.

'So, what did you make of the palace?' the teacher asked them all.

Kay spoke for the first time that day. 'I liked the room with the birdcages. I liked the actors.' She heard her own voice fluting out from the back of the group. But the teacher did not seem to hear her. As if she was not there, the pupils waited in silence for someone else to speak.

Pony

'Look,' Declan said.

Joanna moved to the living room window, from which she could see the back green, the bright square of it.

'Oh,' she said. Her pony was munching grass under the washing line.

'Bloody hell,' he said. 'Some nutcase has gone and got themselves a horse.'

'Looks like it.'

'What were they thinking?'

The thing was, she'd pitied it, all plastered in mud and roped to a lamp post.

'Maybe they didn't think, maybe they just did it,' she said.

The pony walked under a low-slung bath towel. Its shadow created a cut-out shape. He heaved the window open and let in the gentle sound of teeth tearing grass. 'Idiots. They'll not be able to keep it.'

'How'd you know?'

'You can't keep a feckin' horse in a shared garden.'

'It's more a pony,' she said.

Dinner smells and radio noise rose from the other flats.

'How did they even get it here?'

It had clopped along the pavement. Only once stopping to eat questionable flowers. 'I don't know,' she said. Its forlornness had spoken to her of vocation.

'They're expensive,' he said.

'Probably won't cost more than a big dog.'

He turned to her. 'You're not going to start moaning at me for a bleeding dog again?'

'Honestly, no.'

'Good. I worry dogs lead to babies.' He pinched her arm, leaving a white patch.

'Ow. I'm over dogs, and I'll never get on to babies. I've got finer things to think about nowadays.'

They stepped away from the window and headed into their nook of a kitchen where nothing was cooking.

Out back, the pony shook its mane full of sun, and its silhouette shivered. Other figures gathered at other windows. They gazed at the animal the way they would have gazed at a bonfire.

Lily

Lily had taken her name from the bible. He had found this out from one of the other women. Her real name was Laura, but she had chosen Lily about five years ago. *Consider the lillies, how they grow; they neither toil nor spin.* He watched her as she drove. A tiny green gemstone necklace glittering below her throat. Whenever they turned a tight corner, she sucked on her lower lip. She always wore her hair scraped back so that her temples were bare and only a few strands escaped and curled about her ears.

'Did you get your boiler fixed?' she asked out of the silence.

'Nah, not got anything sorted yet.' Outside the car window rust coloured bracken blurred by.

'You should complain. I'd be going nuts by now. Your clothes will go mouldy if you're drying them about the flat with no heating on.'

'I probably wouldn't notice.' He glanced to see if she smiled, but she didn't. Sometimes with her, Fred became aware of the timbre of his voice. Not masculine enough, too pinched.

The car nosed down into a dip then rose again. The grey-tiled roof of a modern house appeared from behind a ridge. The sight of it gave his stomach an uneven feeling. The car slowed, and Lily turned at the drive. 'Here we go.' She parked, and they climbed out, Lily pulling her shoulder bag on. He followed her quick scissor steps. He wondered why they trusted him to go out with her on his own. He had only been at the mission for three months. What did they know about him, really? They had seen a thin slice of temper once, the time he lost it over hot coffee spilt on his lap. But they hardly knew a thing.

She tapped the doorknocker twice. There were sounds in the hallway, clatterings, then the door opened and a woman's face appeared – middle-aged, freckly, bordered by soft spirals of grey and brown hair. Just like before, he found it was bearable once someone was standing there, only another human being after all. The woman gave Lily a confused smile.

'Can I help you?'

'How are you today?' Lily asked.

'I'm well. What's this about?'

'We were wondering if you would let us take a moment to talk to you about God,' Lily said. He watched the woman's smile melt away as he knew it would.

'Ah, no, I think I'm alright, thank you.'

'We'd only take a minute.'

'I'm fine, thanks.' A small boy sat on thick-carpeted stairs behind her, watching them both. A row of different sized shoes lined the corridor.

'Would you take some leaflets?' Lily handed a bunch of about ten through the gap in the door. The woman's hand closed around the pamphlets even as she frowned at them.

'Thank you, thanks, I'd better be getting on... bye now,' and she was pushing the door closed.

'Goodbye,' said Lily through the last remaining crack.

'Bye,' Fred said though the door was already shut.

And that was it. He could almost taste the shame of it, but he turned to Lily and said, 'She'll maybe read them.'

'Maybe.'

'Up to God, I suppose.'

'Yeah, up to God.' Her voice seemed slightly sarcastic.

They got in the car and backed down onto the road and set off again. As they drew closer to the sea, they came to flat pastureland dotted with grazing black-faced sheep. He wondered if they thought anything about the car, the coloured shape rattling by. It was the kind of daft question he guessed other people wouldn't think about. A few ewes had wandered into the road. Lily slowed for them. Their piebald legs and swaying backends. Lily's profile serene beside him. He thought of her soul somewhere inside her head, controlling the precise movements of her eyes and hands. He wanted to reach out and touch the green necklace, circle the space of skin underneath it.

He would not let a strange man go out in a car to the middle of nowhere with a woman like Lily if he was running a mission. The first two times he had gone out with Angus, who talked to him drearily most of the way about football but became another person once he was inside a house; open, exuberant. Fred didn't have a license so he was always paired with a driver. This time, Lily had somehow been left with him, the two of them standing in the hall like the last uncoupled kids at the school disco, until she said, 'Looks like we're a pair.'

From the first time he saw her, he knew that sleeping with her would be like getting a hold on the world somehow, like finding a centre to the bleak whirling earth. He'd been planning how he might ask her out. Yet the reality of sitting next to her solid, warm body in the car made his thoughts jangle and collide.

He had come to the mission on a dripping spring day when things were just about as low as they ever got. Two days before, he'd got into a shoving match with an ex-squaddie at the bookies without knowing how it had happened. The beginning of it was an absolute blank. There was a rage under his skin most people couldn't sense. If he wasn't angry, he appeared meek, he knew that. In the mission, he had sat in one of the faded chairs at the back and felt, not a revelation, but a kind of blotting out. The blotting out was, in that moment, what he had to have, and he ascribed it somehow to the words of the preacher and also to an odd sort of warmth that had seemed to come up through the floorboards and into the soles of his feet. He'd actually asked if they had underfloor heating, it was so real a sensation, but they'd said no, they weren't that posh.

He brought his attention back to the car. 'You're quiet today,' he tried. Before speaking to her each time, he shifted himself upwards inside his own body.

'Och, to be honest, I'm not feeling so good,' she said, her eyes on the road. 'Don't mind me keeping quiet. I'll be glad when today's done.' Perhaps she was saying that only because she did not want to talk to him. The thought brought up a flux of anger that he had to swallow. He made a silent prayer to conduct himself right. Sometimes he felt like God was on his side, and sometimes he perceived God as a force against him. Other times it seemed obvious that there was no God.

The next house became visible. A low, grey stone cottage with bursts of steam coming out of a side-pipe like smoke signals. They pulled into the drive, over-grown with pale, wiry grass. There were children's things on the lawn, a red and blue slide and a daisy-patterned paddling pool full of leaves and dirt. This talking to strangers about religion was a kind of penance for him; it humiliated him in a way few other things could.

They rang the bell. A girl in a polka-dot dress opened the door part way.

'Hello. I hope you're well today. Can you take a minute to talk about God?' Lily began. He was thinking they should ask the girl if her parents were in, but he realised she must be older than she appeared. She had a pleasant, pudgy look about her face like a pouch-cheeked rodent. Her eyelids were coated with smoky make-up that made them seem to droop.

'Oh, I don't really have time just now, but I am a Christian and that.' Her expression switched from sincere to amused and back to sincere inside a moment.

'Well, that's a good start. What does being a Christian mean to you?'

There was a pause of a few beats. 'You know, what it means to everyone. I go to church and stuff sometimes.'

'Do you pray?'

'Sure, when I'm worried about something.' Again sincere, amused, sincere.

'That's great, but you could also pray when things are going well. Prayers of thanksgiving,' Lily said.

'Sure. Listen, I don't really have time to talk just now, though, so...'

A noise of pans came from the kitchen.

'Is there anyone else in who might like to talk with us?' Lily asked.

'No, I'm on my own.' The noise came again from the kitchen but the girl didn't blink.

'What's your name?'

'Heather.' The girl's mouth twitched for a second as she said it, and he wondered if she'd made that up on the spot. The girl was slight. He could imagine picking her up and slinging her over his shoulder.

'Heather, are you sure you couldn't spare a few moments to talk to us a little more?'

'Sorry, no.'

'OK then, we'll let you get on, but it sounds like you are on the right track, don't give up now. We'll leave these leaflets with you.' Lily's hand reached out with a bundle of papers. He was leaving her to do the talking again, but she seemed to just keep rolling out the words as if they were printed on a strip inside her eyes.

'Thanks,' the girl said, taking them. As the door closed, he shifted back to believing she was as young as he first thought, maybe thirteen or fourteen.

They returned to the car, Lily's gestures flowing even in the way she put her belt on, checked her reflection in the mirror. Some days, when she left the mission in the afternoon, headed down the alleyway and out, he had the urge to grab her wrist, to clamp hold of it so that they couldn't be parted, so that his hand became a kind of manacle.

Now the sky above the distant mountains opened, and the sun highlighted a section of rock. White beams splitting through the cloud resembling the kind of light he saw representing God on the front of the tattered books on the mission bookshelf. For a few seconds, looking directly at the light, he felt that sense of being blotted out.

They drove through moorland without houses, marked by long flat rocks and isolated boulders. He caught flashes of his reflection in the wing mirror, his silvering hair. He'd never asked Lily's age, but he must have a decade on her. The land began to dip and offer glimpses of the sea loch through young silver birches. The car heated up until it contained a thick warmth. He was aware of Lily's thigh near his hand, wrapped tightly in her jeans. He imagined her skin under her clothes. And then without wanting to, deeper than that, the muscles and sinews. He dug his fingers into his palms. He imagined the atoms inside the sinews. Her eyes were fixed on the road. She had not looked at him since the house. Then, from nothing, she glanced at him and gave him a little smile. It was infuriating and beautiful. He found himself speaking.

'Do you want to go for food when we're back in town? We could go to that new Chinese place.'

Before he had time to think about whether he'd made a mistake, she was answering, 'No, I don't think so, I'm not in much of a mood for eating today. Just feeling a bit green round the gills.'

The landscape seemed to darken at her answer. Was she saying no to that particular meal, or was she saying no to him? A memory like a short piece of film blinked into his head. There was Angus patting the small of her back as they arrived at the mission that morning. Her smiling a wider, more open smile than she'd had for him all day. Maybe they were actually together, and he had failed to notice. He recalled another time when a visiting preacher had shown a projector presentation. Lily had taken one of the plastic chairs at the side, and Angus had come round and sat on the floor in front of her. She had rested her foot on his shoulder for a moment, and he'd joked about her socks smelling.

Two wooden houses appeared below them. They took a route off to the side, circled down. Lily parked the car. She didn't look at him as he got out. There was the acidic taste of anger again; he observed it rising.

They reached the first of two houses, and Lily rang the doorbell. Through the glass panel, he saw a wavering figure approaching like someone appearing from underwater. The door swung back. A woman stood in a padded green waistcoat, wiping flour from her hands with a checked dishcloth. 'What is it?' The house had a smell like almonds.

'How are you this afternoon?' Lily said.

'What do you want?'

'Can we talk to you for a minute about God?'

The woman broke into a smile that showed a row of small, rounded teeth. She had a dash of flour on her left cheek like a streak of lightning. 'No, you may not.'

'You might find it's worth your while,' Lily said.

'You two might find it worth your while to get jobs.'

'I have a job,' said Lily.

The woman's face became dappled pink like a baby's. 'Go on, bugger off. There was a guy round last week as well. Was he one of yours? Stop bothering folk with your ugly nonsense.' The woman waved her hand, and Lily took a step backwards.

'Have a pleasant day,' Lily managed before the door slammed.

She turned and started walking towards the next house, her body angled forward. The garden of this one was full of gnomes and potted plants. When he caught up with her, he could see she was grinning. Her eyes flashed sideways and met his, and he grinned back at her. He felt soaked through with light from her gaze, like a tiny gift from God. 'You keep very cool,' he said. She shrugged, still smiling, but her fingers pulled at a strand of hair.

'They despise us. I don't let myself feel small,' she said. What was her job anyway? He thought she worked in a pharmacy. She had spoken of it, and he had not listened.

They rang the next doorbell and stood on the porch a few minutes, but no one came. A large dog barked from somewhere inside the house, sounding as if it was deep in a cave. Further out, through the cow field, a whitewashed, traditional farmhouse stood beside a low metal shed.

'Let's try that one,' Lily said.

They reached a gate; it was chained up in a complicated way. They wrangled with the fastening then decided to climb over it, Lily first.

'Hope there's no bull,' she said, landing with a little jump like a gymnast. He climbed over in a few steps. The cows had new, velvety calves meandering amongst their legs.

'They wouldn't put the bull in when they've got their young,' he said.

They walked through the field together. The cows lifted their heads, turned their gaze on them, their chewing slowed. The calves copied, dark sparkling eyes. As they got halfway along the tractor path, the animals began to move in their direction. Within a minute, the bulk of the herd was a few feet away. He scanned for the massive head of a bull among the group of them. 'It's OK, they're all females,' he said. 'They probably think we're going to feed them.' More came to block the road in front, all staring. He didn't like the way they loomed, but he wanted to sound calm.

'Let's go back,' Lily said. 'They'll not let us through.'

'They'll not do anything,' he said.

They took a few steps more. He heard crunching stones behind them on the path. He looked round, there were cows to the back of them now too. The nearest one, a dappled grey, let out a bellow so loud he flinched.

'I don't like this,' Lily said. Her eyes darted about. The animals had formed a lopsided ring around them.

'None of them are bulls,' he repeated. He made a shooing motion with his arms. 'Bugger off.' But the beasts stood their ground, four or five of them making low, loud calls. He'd never really noticed how big cows were, the sheer bulk of them.

'They think we want to take their calves,' Lily said.

'Nah, they just want food from us.'

His left foot slipped, and he righted himself. He flapped the sides of his coat. A couple of the animals lowered their heads threateningly. 'Don't,' Lily said. 'You're upsetting them. How are we going to get out?' Her voice was rising in pitch.

'We'll just walk through them,' he said. But he didn't move, and neither did she. The mud suctioning at his shoes.

A gap appeared at the side of the circle, and Lily dashed towards it, and at the same time, a piebald calf tripped into the space so it seemed that she was running at it. The grey cow nearest lowered its head and took a few quick paces at her as if it meant to charge. Lily yipped and turned back.

'They're going for us,' she said. 'I don't feel well. I don't like this.' She was becoming tearful.

'Don't panic.' He turned to look for another gap. He should be able to fight his way out, but they frightened him with their black staring eyes.

A tiny tug. There was an inquisitive muzzle chewing at his sleeve, and in the split second of surprise, his elbow thwacked back against the calf's nose. Seconds later, he was hit from behind with a force that shocked him. He fell forward and struggled up as quickly as he could. He turned. A reddish cow had butted him, its head still lowered. It was standing near, and he could guess it had used only a fraction of its strength.

He looked over at Lily. Her eyes were wide. To her side, there was a space opening up again, and now she made a dash towards it. The cows stayed steady, watching her. She was in the gap when the same red cow charged her. She tried to swerve back, but it connected with her side. She screamed, slipped and fell, and it circled past her. He took a step forward to help her, but the red cow made its way back and stood over her. Other cows scattered and regrouped. He smelt their fermenting breath. They were going to crush her, in front of him. He would have to see and hear it all. He couldn't move. His rage was nowhere. His legs were rooted. Lily's face was bathed in panic. She raised her arms to protect her skull. At the same moment a voice called out, 'Get on, go on with you now.' A man in wellies clapping his hands above his head. The cow standing over Lily galloped off, barely missing her face with its back hooves. The herd dispersed.

'What the hell are you doing to my cows?' the man said. Lily got up clumsily. One side of her was painted with mud. 'Eh? Where are you going? There's nothing but the farmhouse at the end of this track.' Fred wanted to tell him to go fuck himself, that he could have spooked the cow into kicking Lily's head, but he didn't say anything. The rage wouldn't take light.

'We were just walking,' Lily said.

'Well, why don't you just walk on back to your car? You've terrified my cows. They're with their calves.'

'We were about to leave,' Lily said, turning.

Fred tried to take her forearm but she snatched it away. It had been so easy for the farmer to make the cows run. Fred could have scattered them himself if he'd charged them, made his own bellowing. They returned to the gate, squelching through the mud. The cows stayed away from them, uninterested now. Some started to graze.

He and Lily began climbing the gate, balancing on the rungs.

'Open it properly! You're wrecking the bloody hinges,' the man shouted from across the field, but they carried on. Lily dropped down over the bar, Fred followed. He reached out to offer his arm again, but she appeared not to notice.

'I feel like puking,' she said.

They returned to the car. Lily put some newspaper on their seats to protect them from the mud. 'You can brush most of the mud off when it dries,' he said. They got in and did up their belts. She clasped the wheel, flexed her fingers, and turned to him.

'Onwards.' Her voice jokingly gung-ho, but with a tightness to it.

They got back onto the road by the sea loch. Light ticked over them from between the trees. He waited a while before speaking.

'I guess that was kind of funny, in a way,' he offered.

'I don't trust cows,' she said, unsmiling. 'They're used to having their calves taken off them. That's why they went for us. They don't trust us either.'

'I think they were just hoping for food. I'm sorry you fell.'

'Never mind,' she said, frowning. There was his rage now, to think that he had been frozen, and she'd seen it and might despise him.

They drove in silence. He had the urge to ask her out again, almost push her to reject him flatly. She was pale, though. Like a vampire had been at her. In a way, that was satisfying because it meant maybe she was ill and had not been lying before. They reached a section of road where the trees ended and the sea view opened out and the water reached unblemished to one of the Inner Hebrides, he wasn't sure which. 'Are you feeling better?' he said.

'No, to be honest.'

'Want to go back?'

'We're as quick doing the full loop now,' she said. They were reaching the remotest edge.

They carried on driving, seeing no houses. Lily made little murmuring noises occasionally.

'Feeling sick?'

'Yes.'

'Want to stop for a bit?'

'No.'

Finally, a bungalow appeared ahead of them, up on a bare slope looking out to the horizon with its dim, square eyes. No car was waiting by it. They drove up anyway, stalling on the driveway before pulling up beside the painted yellow front door. A pink shirt and two pairs of jeans made human movements on the washing line.

They clambered out, approached the door. She rang the bell. The wind whipped at their hair and clothes. He pressed the buzzer a second time, it echoed, and no one came.

'Away, I suppose,' he said. Lily didn't speak. She turned and headed back to the car and sat in the driver's seat. It made him ache, the way she folded away her long legs. He walked round to his side and opened the door. He said a quick prayer, joining the tips of his fingers.

'When I asked if you wanted to eat together, y'know, I was really asking you out. Would you go out with me sometime?'

Her mouth tightened. 'No, oh no, Fred. No.' She opened her door and turned to the side. There was a faint sucking in of breath, then she said, 'I'm going to be sick.' She spat heavily. Coughed, gagged. Fury, clotting in his throat. He wanted to take her shoulders and shake her so that her head snapped back, so that her teeth clicked together.

He got up, out of the car, and walked round the empty house. The first formed sting in his mind was a sense that she was being physically sick because of him, because he'd asked her out. But, no, that was too much. She must be ill, as she said. He came to the back of the house. The garden was only a trimmed lawn and an empty whirligig. He looked hotly into the dark windows and had the odd sensation that a creature mirroring his anger might be hunkered down on the floor glaring back out at him. He'd broken someone's fingers for laughing at him once. He put his hands to the glass and stared in at the reflection of his own eyes, huge and grey. He could see through himself into the house. A patterned carpet and building block toys. Then the words *morning sickness* came floating into his head. He imagined grabbing Angus by the neck of his shirt, lifting him off the ground, the surprise on his silly, smooth face. *Morning sickness.*

He stalked further round the house and looked into a bedroom. It was bare except for a single bed with perfect white sheets on it. As if it had never been touched by anyone, which disturbed him. Like the contents of the house only existed as a kind of display. He returned to the car kicking at pebbles. He had in mind that he would ask if she was pregnant.

He stood by his door. She was slumped back on the seat. There was a thin veil of sweat over her face and neck, giving it a sheen like a pony's coat in summer. 'I'm so hot,' she said quietly. She was no longer pale but flushed. Something seemed to turn in the crown of his head. She was surely too ill for morning sickness. Did that cause this kind of lethargy and blankness, this heat? A blot of triumph even as he sensed the danger. She might not be pregnant. It might be some virus, some bug, some problem inside her.

They had no signal on their phones out here. He looked about him. The sea was silent, periwinkle blue, too far down the hill to make a sound. He could not drive. He took his phone out to check it though he knew there'd be nothing. No bars.

She was gasping, taking the air too fast like a dehydrated person gulping water. She looked as if she might pass out. He reached over and carefully touched his fingers to her cheek. Hot.

'Don't, please don't,' she said. He kept his hand there for a minute, then drew it back.

'You're really not well, are you?' he said, and she didn't reply. He gave up a silent prayer again, fingertips touching. He looked around. Help should come now, some sign, some guidance. A doe was watching them from the far bank. He didn't point it out to Lily; her eyes were closed. The doe flinched like a shy dog, turned and vanished.

Lily was not well. His mind was unsnarled now. He would stay beside her until help materialised, and then she would be grateful. She would owe him something. She would be his yet. A car would appear round the bend in a minute or two. It was such a sure feeling, he clung onto it as if it was a lump of clay he could dig his fingers into. He sat in the seat next to her and stroked her forehead and she moaned.

'Don't,' she said. 'Don't touch me.' God, she was white like her name. He smoothed the hair at her temple with the crook of his finger. 'Help me,' she said, but she was looking away then, not asking him for help but someone unseen. 'Don't.' She shifted in her chair. 'Help, help.'

He waited for assistance to come as the slow seconds passed, watching the sea, watching the shivering grass, watching the black coil of road. All he had to do was sit and wait. Watching the road, the sea, the grass, the sky. Studying the line of her throat and the sweat on her face and the glints of the little green necklace.

Wormholes

The aliens looked like skittles at a bowling alley, he said.
They'd appeared in the night, pale and standing in a row
at the end of his bed.

On her first day, Emily was introduced to the four residents
by Priya, another support worker. The flat was set up to ac-
commodate adults with learning disabilities and complex
needs. There were four small en-suite bedrooms, a kitchen, a
living room and a scrap of balcony. Emily met Toby last; he
was sitting at the foldout table in the kitchen, wearing a blue
shirt, the sleeves buttoned up with silver cufflinks.

'Toby hasn't had breakfast because he's been a lazybones
and slept in. Toby, could you show Emily where the breakfast
things are to help her get settled?'

'That would be great,' said Emily. 'What are you planning
to have for breakfast, sir?'

Toby looked at her, twirling a butter knife. 'Prawns.'

'You eat prawns for breakfast?'

A smile blossomed. 'Just joking.'

'What will you really have?'

'Sardines.'

'Seriously?'

'No, joking. Toast. With strawberry jam.'

'Alright. Maybe you could show me how you like to make it?'

Unhurried, he drew himself up and retrieved a loaf from a flowery breadbin, opened a cupboard and pointed to a stack of small plates. 'Toby has trouble with his hands,' Priya said. 'It's something in the joints. You need to help him get the plates down.'

Toby looked at Emily with lucid blue eyes. 'You having breakfast?'

'I've already had thanks, I'm full up. Want me to put the bread in the toaster for you?'

Toby shook his head. 'He can put the slices in himself,' Priya said, 'but spread the jam for him. You'll make a scutter otherwise, won't you?' Toby nodded seriously. He picked two slices out of the packet and dropped them into the toaster. The kitchen looked out onto a car park, the sun sliding in cream bands between the surrounding houses. When the toast popped up, Toby clattered the slices onto a plate, and Emily opened the jam with some difficulty.

'So, what do you think of Emily? Is she nice?' Priya asked him.

'She's nice. And gullible,' he said, watching her spread the jam as if she might well go wrong.

Apart from Toby, the occupants in the supported living flat were a young man and an older woman who both had autism combined with a learning disability, and Bella, a woman of thirty-five with Down's syndrome. Toby was in his fifties and had no specific diagnosis other than developmental delay. 'He was sleeping rough in the eighties,' Priya said, 'then he some-how ended up in a grim institutional place for a lot of years.

After that, he was moved into community care. Nothing much else is known about his background.'

Toby told Emily about the aliens on her third shift. He said they'd appeared during the night, the last summer gone. 'While I was in my bed.'

'Was it a dream?'

'No, real.'

'Did they take you into their ship?' Emily said, guessing it was one of his games.

'No, just looked at me. Three of them. Had big eyes. They were pretty.'

'Pretty? Were they women?'

'No,' he said. 'They looked like... like... what you get at the bowling alley?'

'Bowling balls?'

'No. Things you knock over.'

'Skittles?'

'Yeah, skittles. And they were glowing. Like light bulbs,'

One of the other support workers, Nick, wandered in then, carrying four overstuffed bags of groceries. 'I don't think Emily wants to hear your alien story.'

'I do, actually. It's really interesting.'

The bags rustled and clinked as Nick put them on the countertop. He often seemed to be in a bad mood. In a cartoon, he would have been followed around by a plump, grey raincloud. *Nick's a bit of an arse*, Priya had said, without any sense of animosity.

Emily's shifts rotated through the days of the week like a spinning wheel. She did not work nights and only saw the sleepover staff as she was leaving. She came to like Toby best, his humour and calmness. On a Sunday morning, she washed the dishes while Toby finished his cereal. The residents were supposed to help with the chores, but often the staff just did it all for quickness. Toby had a cut-out picture of a woman from a magazine, a radiant face from an advert for yogurt, which he was turning round beside his bowl as if it was a puzzle.

'Is she your girlfriend?' Emily asked.

He looked at her like she was stupid. 'No.'

'I'm joking,' she said, but he didn't laugh.

When she reached to take away his tea mug, he said, 'I had a boyfriend once, but he left me for a girl who worked in a laundry.'

'Well, he was silly,' she said, tipping the half-inch of cold tea down the sink. 'You're very handsome.'

She didn't know why she'd said that. He wasn't handsome. One of his front teeth stood out yellow as butter, overlapping another, and his woolly grey hair was arranged in tufts so that he was bald in unexpected patches.

'You must miss him,' she said.

'Don't want to talk about it.' He rotated the picture of the woman again so that her smile turned upside down.

She put the last dish into the rack. 'You could help me with the drying.'

'Dishes dry themselves,' he said.

Toby could take showers or baths without assistance, but whenever he did, a staff member had to sit outside the bathroom door on a plastic chair. Afterwards, they had to help Toby do up any buttons. He always liked to wear his cufflinks and complained if they couldn't be found. The policy around baths and showers had tightened since the agency had been involved in the death of a woman with epilepsy five years ago.

Emily often volunteered to sit outside the bathroom. Because she couldn't leave her post, she was free to read a magazine and let her thoughts drift, tuning in only to the occasional safe, lapping sound of water in the background. Nick laughed at her magazines. She chose the cheap ones full of real-life stories, the kind made of rustly paper with ink that came off on her fingers. Several times Nick walked past, squinting at the cover headlines and reading them out loud. *'He left me for my twin on my wedding night. My sister was my mother.'* She took to folding the magazines into quarters to hide the story titles.

One Monday morning, Emily was helping Bella into her new spring coat when Priya arrived through the door with Toby.

'Where were you today?' Emily asked him.

'Doctors,' he said.

'All go alright?' she asked.

'I'm dying.'

Pausing with Bella's arm halfway into her sleeve, she scanned Priya's face. Priya shook her head.

'Is that true, Toby?'

'Nope,' he said, raising his chin. He was sporting a few shaving cuts today.

'He has athlete's foot,' said Priya, 'which is funny because I can hardly get him to walk down the stairs. You'll never make an athlete, pal.' Priya poked him in the ribs, and he started laughing.

Bella smiled nervously, arms by her sides in the powder blue coat she had chosen for herself on a recent shopping trip. She was often flustered by loud laughter, alert to the possibility of being teased.

. . .

'I have a son,' Toby said one day after lunch. The television was on in the sitting room, the others watching a grainy cowboy film. Occasional muted shots rang out. Despite his reputation for laziness, Toby did not like to sit in front of the TV.

'A son?' Emily asked.

'Yes. I had a girlfriend, she had a baby.'

'I thought you liked guys?'

'Yeah. But when I was young. I had a girlfriend. She had a boy. They took him off her.'

'Toby, that's really sad. If it's true.'

He nodded. 'It was bad. I couldn't stop it.' A horse whinnied from the television. The clopping of hooves, or coconut halves.

Later she asked Priya about the baby. 'Far as I know, it's true. Someone did a bit of tracing a while back. I think the mother had a learning disability too. They usually took any kids away in those days.'

Toby told Emily about the aliens so often that it started to seem like something she had seen in a picture book long ago. She had in mind a solid, black and white image of bottle-necked creatures lined up at the end of the quilt, shimmering and benign, like angels surrounding a deathbed. He'd said they were kind. She'd asked how he knew that, and he'd said he could feel it in his belly.

When she was little, Emily watched documentaries about alien encounters with her brother. The stories were always told directly by the experiencer. The people had usually been in a car on an empty backroad surrounded by open fields of grain. They saw the spacecraft first, a light like a candle flame detached from its wick. Sometimes the experiencer claimed they were beamed into the craft, other times it all happened on the ground. After their story, the programme would cut to a sceptic to explain how the account couldn't be real. As a child, Emily was sceptical of the sceptics. Next, the show would bring on someone with wild hair and a bow tie, introduced as a scientist, who would discuss why the stories were, in fact, very plausible.

Emily and her brother would watch, sitting side by side on the old brown couch, eating jelly beans from a packet. The memory came with the sensation of a diamond in her throat, hard and clear.

On a Friday afternoon shift in April, she arrived to find Toby looking at bits of plants with a magnifying glass. The kitchen window was open, and a buzzing noise came from outside, like a strimmer far away or a bees' nest close by. She was pleased by the idea that there were bees out there, a colony of alien-shaped creatures.

'Hello. How are you today?' she said to Toby.

'Fine. Bella's dead, though.'

'What?'

'She died this morning,' he said, gazing down. The plant pieces were laid out on a paper towel, dissected into stems and leaves and petals.

'Are you joking?' she stepped into the kitchen. A drum began to beat in her ears.

'No,' he shook his head. 'Died first thing.'

'Seriously?'

'Yes.'

The drum beat louder. She reached the corner of the table, and from there, she could see into the living room. The flickering of the television. Bella was sitting on the edge of the couch, watching an animal cartoon, eating crisps from a tube. Her favourite cuddly toy pony was balanced on the armrest.

'Toby, Bella is right there.'

Still looking through the magnifying glass, he grinned.

Emily moved around and stood beside him. 'Toby, it's not funny to say people have died when they haven't. Poor Bella. That isn't a joke.' He ignored her and kept smiling down at his plant pieces like he was watching something scurrying around inside them.

Later, she wondered about the phrasing. *Died first thing.* First thing in the morning. It could be a real sentence someone had said to Toby once, breaking the news about a death in his life. Or he could have just plucked the phrase from the air.

'How are you getting on with Toby's stories?' Nick asked her as they were helping Bella make a cake.

'I think I'm getting better at working out what's true and what isn't,' Emily said. 'Like, there's a few things he says which are consistent. The stuff about him having a boyfriend who left him for a laundry girl.'

'Yeah, that one's true. I used to take them to the cinema together years back. They'd always spend a fortune on wine gums and liquorice.'

'Poor Toby, he must have been gutted when it ended.'

'He was. He stopped eating for a while.'

'How'd you get him to start again?'

'I told him to stop being such a pain in the arse.'

She ignored this, tipped flour onto the scale. After a bit, she asked, 'How long have you worked here then?'

'Oh, forever,' Nick said.

She reached to put the flour bag back in the cupboard, spilling a thin trail.

'And the one about there having been a baby? That's true?'

'Yes. A social worker traced the boy years back.' He lowered his voice. 'The boy wavered on whether to meet Toby, but in the end, he wrote a letter saying he'd decided against contact, and that was that.'

'God, how sad. Does Toby understand?'

'We explained as best we could.'

Bella began patting at the flour trail with a damp cloth. 'Thanks, Bella. Poor Toby. Jesus. I guess an actual meeting could go so many ways.'

'There's that. How would you feel, finding out Toby was your biological father?'

This question left her dangling, feet off the ground. She was going to say she'd be fine about it, then that it wasn't a fair question. 'I... I don't know. I mean, of course... I don't know.'

They worked silently for a while, then she said, 'You know, the alien story is consistent too. He's quite passionate about that one.'

'Yeah, but obviously that's not real.'

'Well, you never know.' She turned. 'Want to lick the spoon?' Bella took it from her and ran her tongue along it.

'How could the alien thing be true?' Nick said.

'Life is weird.'

'Don't you think people would notice a great big fucking spacecraft landing in the car park behind the flats?' Bella glanced at him with widened eyes. She had the most graceful eyelashes.

'OK. Yeah,' Emily said. 'But we don't know everything. I mean, there's wormholes...'

'What about wormholes?'

'Well. Mmm. Couldn't they... I mean, I don't know,' she said, tipping two tablespoons of sugar into the icing bowl, looking back to see his forehead gathering lines.

'God, fucking wormholes. It's what people who don't understand science say when they want to believe in something ridiculous. Just say 'wormholes', and that means there's aliens or an afterlife. It's a stupid person's idea of science.' He turned to look at her. He had a tiny mole on his neck that she had never noticed before. 'I mean, I'm thinking of people in the public eye not bothering to research anything. I wasn't saying that you're stupid.'

'Yeah. Except that you kind of did. But it's fine,' she said. She folded over the sugar bag and wedged it back into the cupboard. Bella was mixing the bowl again with the licked spoon. 'Why do you do this job?' she asked him.

'Why do you?'

'Because I saw it advertised. And I needed paid work, and I was just about qualified for it.'

'Well, same reason,' he said.

Except that wasn't the whole of her reason. When she was little, she'd had a dolls' house with electric lights that could be flicked on and off. She'd often close it all up and kneel in front of it and look through the lit window frames, half expecting one of the dolls to move. In a way she couldn't explain, the reason for wanting the job was connected to the sensation of peering into the miniature windows.

'What do you think about the aliens?' she asked Priya when they were alone a few days later. She found she'd begun to imagine wormholes popping up all over the city in her day-to-day life. Wormholes, as she pictured them, were like canvas tunnels leading to other places. Whenever she was walking down Princes Street now, she imagined one appearing with a sucking noise in the middle of the pavement and gobbling up a few shoppers and tourists.

'You mean Toby's extra-terrestrials?'

'Yeah.'

They were folding clothes from the laundry side by side.

'It's probably not real,' Priya said.

'But there could be something to it, couldn't there? How do you really know for sure about anything like that?'

'I don't know, but the idea creeps me out.'

'I find it sort of comforting. To think there's more.'

'More what?'

'More to life.'

'Nick thinks it's a kind of waking dream,' Priya began folding a spotted bath towel. 'Hypnogog something.'

'Nick doesn't know everything.'

'Yeah, but he is very smart. You should see his bookshelves. They're full of really thick books, fat as bricks.'

'That doesn't make him clever,' Emily said. 'They could be big books full of crap. Maybe he hasn't even read them.'

'Well, the spines are all lined at least.'

'Maybe they're from charity shops,' Emily said. She'd made a mess of folding a pillowcase, so she shook it out and began again. 'So, why were you at his flat?'

Priya looked at her and laughed. 'Oh, it's not like that. He's got a girlfriend.'

'Has he?'

'Yeah, she's a lawyer or something. An attorney or an advocate or an actuary or one of those.'

'Oh right, he's never mentioned. Why were you round his flat then?'

'Because we're friends.' Priya had got an eyebrow newly pierced with a small gold stud, a tiny star. Or had it always been like that, and she was only seeing it now?

'I thought you said he's an arse.'

'He is. Doesn't mean we're not friends. He's a bit of a poor thing, really. Besides, eighty per cent of my friends are arse-holes, I don't hold it against them. Not you, though. You're one of my rare, non-arsehole friends.'

'Thanks,' Emily said. It surprised her that Priya thought of her as a friend. They had never met outside of work. She carried on with her folding. The laundry smelt of synthetic meadows. Later that day, she saw Nick and Priya leaving together, walking side by side down the pavement.

She found herself daydreaming of coming back to the flat to find Toby gone, whisked away by the skittle aliens. *I told you*, she would say to Nick, who would be standing unmoving, rooted to the carpet, with his mouth gaping like a koi carp. Sometimes these scenarios turned nasty in a way she couldn't seem to help imagining. There would be a burned-out gap in the ceiling where Toby had been taken, and Nick would shout at her, *You knew it was real, why did you let it happen?*

One clear evening when a blackbird was singing next to the kitchen window, trilling and improvising, Toby told her the aliens had been again.

'Three of them?'

'Three. They had nice music.'

'Can you remember it?'

'Yes,' he said. He pinched in his lips and started to hum Somewhere Over the Rainbow.

'That's the music the aliens had?'

'Yeah.' Tapping the table with his fingernails.

'Toby, that's from a film.'

'No it's not.'

'Yes it is. That's from the Wizard of Oz.' A little twist in her solar plexus.

'It's not – it was real,' he said, blinking hard.

'Toby, that music is from the Wizard of Oz, you must have seen it.' She brought her face down to his. His breath today smelt like milk drying round the lip of a bottle. He didn't move away but glared back at her.

'Not a film, I heard it,' he said.

'Have you been making all this up about the aliens?'

'No, it was real! It was real!' He looked out the window and then gave a sudden chuckle. He resumed humming Somewhere Over the Rainbow.

'You can't just lie all the time, Toby,' she said in a way that stopped the humming.

He pressed his hands down flat on the tabletop, gulping. 'I don't.'

'But you do, you do, everyone knows you do.'

He stared at her. 'Don't.'

'Yes, you do!'

'I don't.'

'You're always bloody lying.'

Nick came in. 'What's wrong?'

'Nothing,' she said.

'You were raising your voice to him.'

'I was not. We were just talking.' Toby looked away from her. She expected Nick to say something more, but he didn't. Instead he took a cloth and began wiping the kitchen surfaces. Toby started laughing again, tipping backwards like he was on a fairground ride.

. . .

A locked cabinet sat in the far corner of the living room. In it, they kept paper files on each of the residents, medical records and legal documents. One day, she was looking through it for Toby's date of birth, and she found a picture of a teenage boy wearing a school uniform paper-clipped to a letter headed with a charity name, *Action on Adoption*. She took it out and studied the face. The boy was smiling and holding a violin. He had fluffy hair that stood up like a popstar's. There seemed to be something of Toby's nose and chin, something in the way the eyes crinkled. Or was she imagining that? On the back was written, *'This is me.'* She held the picture, turned it left and right. In the end, she looked at it for so long that the features stopped making sense. She slid it back into the drawer.

In the last week of May, she came in carrying daffodils. She'd woken that morning to the sound of the rubbish truck outside her shutters. The flashing lights and noise had made her think that her room was being invaded, a mechanical assembly coming to get her. Not the good-natured, bowling-alley aliens but a threatening force, the beginning of the end of the world. After rising, she'd felt slightly sick and had not eaten breakfast. A sense of being shaken and rattled stayed with her. On the way to work, she'd been drawn to buy the daffodils in order to have something natural and harmless in her hand.

'Hello,' she said to Toby when she reached the kitchen. The window was open, the smell of strimmed plants drifting in.

'Flowers,' he said.

'Yup. To brighten up the place.'

'That's nice,' Toby said. 'Nick's died.'

'Not really.'

'Yes, really. He fell over. Like that,' he toppled his hand onto the table, making a smacking noise.

She looked around for Nick. 'Where is he anyway?'

'He's dead.'

'Where?'

'In there,' Toby pointed to the living room.

She turned. The room appeared empty. She stood still for a moment, scanning the doorway. Then she saw that there was a dark shape on the floor at the edge of the couch.

'Toby, I told you not to lie about these things. Why are you saying he's dead?'

'Because he is.'

The air began to fizz.

She took a step forward towards the living room door.

'He fell over,' Toby said from behind her. Her arms and legs were prickling, some kind of energy. She stepped into the room, approaching the couch. She had the thought that a wormhole might be about to open above her and swallow her up.

As she reached the dark shape, it began to take form until she could see that it was a discarded cardigan. She bent to pick it off the ground. Then she heard a rasping noise, like someone taking a terrible, choking breath.

Everything in the room looked highly detailed: the ribbed couch fabric, the bobbling texture of the carpet, the purple lint on the skirting board. Her blood running hot, she turned.

It was the balcony door sliding open. Nick stepped into the room, holding a stubbed-out cigarette.

'Hello,' he said. 'Has Toby been telling you I'm dead?'

'Yes, actually.'

'He's been saying that to everyone this morning.'

'You must have done something to piss him off,' she said.

'Not that I'm aware of.'

Nick put his cigarette end in the bin. They were not supposed to use the balcony for smoking. 'I'll tell,' she said. Nick shook his head slightly, meaning he didn't believe her, or he didn't care. His mole was gone. Maybe it had been a smudge of chocolate. They headed back to the kitchen.

'You got a fright,' Toby said, peering at her face.

'No, I didn't.'

'Yes, you did,' Toby said. He stretched out in triumph.

'I didn't. Why would I care if Nick was dead? He's extremely annoying.' She glanced round to see if Nick was smiling, but he had his back to her.

'I'll put some toast on,' he said.

She sat down beside Toby.

'You're a terrible liar,' she said. 'Think of the boy who cried wolf. No one believed him, and he got all eaten up in the end.'

Toby leant in close to her. 'I was joking about Nick,' he whispered, 'but it was real about the music and the aliens.' His eyes were on her, assessing. 'And I had a son. I never saw him – he got taken. I couldn't stop it.'

She almost reached to touch his elbow but drew her hand away. 'Get me some toast too,' she said to Nick over Toby's head. Nick laid out three plates in front of them.

'Nightmare,' Toby said. She wasn't sure if he was talking about the time the baby was taken, or if he was referring to something in the present. Where the will to ask might have been once, there was a blank.

When the toast was ready, she left Toby to spread his own jam, and he got it on his fingers and the tabletop. There was that hard diamond again, right behind her tongue. They ate together in silence, except for the buzzing coming from outside the window. The faraway or nearby hum, halfway between a strimmer and a hidden colony of wild bees.

The Caravan Site

The caravan site was hidden from the main road, along a tractor path through the woods. I loved how thin the walls of our caravan were, like the sides of a tin can. At night, the wild domain was just an inch away. I had a bunk at the back, and my dad slept on the two couches at the front, folded down into a double bed. There was a small gas stove and a kettle that whistled when it began to boil. The caravans on the site were all parked in a circle; ours sat towards the back, near the trees. We were there to wait for the world to end.

Our caravan had an awning where we stored outdoor chairs and spare bedding, BBQ utensils and a child's cricket set that was never used. I ended up leaving odd bits of rubbish lying about as well, crisp packets and the soft drinks bottles I got through. Slugs found their way in and collected around the empty bottles. 'You better start picking those up,' my dad said, but I liked finding the slugs, their different sizes and colours, some pale as ivory, others bright as pieces of amber. At night if you stepped into the awning, you could hear the fizzing of the trees in the wind.

There were seven other children not too far from my age on the site. Also, two babies and an older teenage girl with a butterfly tattoo on her wrist, who mostly spent time with the adults. One family had brought a dog though dogs were not allowed. A chocolate spaniel that never barked. They lied about getting rid of him and kept him hidden in their caravan, the kids from that family walking him late at night with a narrow torch beam.

My dad made our dinners from canned food mainly: tuna, spaghetti alphabets, skinned new potatoes, and corned beef which I had never had before and loved. Occasionally, he drove as far as the village, and we'd buy fresh haddock and fry it and make the caravan stink for days. Much of his other time seemed to be taken up with papers, sifting and sorting. I never knew exactly what they were connected to, although he mentioned an insurance claim.

It was said that the end of the world would begin from the ocean. Fire would crack open the waves. I didn't believe it would happen, but I was content to play along. It was a miracle in and of itself to be away from school. A few weeks into our time at the camp, the couple next door gave us their toaster, and for a while we had all our meals on toast. Alphabet on toast, tuna on toast, corned beef on toast, I ate them all with enthusiasm. The windows of our caravan were tinted brown so that when you returned to the outside world on a sunny day the colours seemed to pop, luminous green grass and a florescent sky, as if the world really was in some strange intermittent state.

My father knew the man in the caravan to our left from a building job he'd had long ago. He spent a lot of time talking to him. Perhaps it was this man who'd persuaded him to join the camp. I'd known my dad was religious in some way, that he attended something called a fellowship now and again. Until this trip, though, announced one weekend when I was over at his house for the beginning of the summer holidays, I did not have any sense that he could believe something like this. No one attempted to get the children to accept the dogma of the camp in great detail, and I chose to take the whole thing as an adventure, as if my father had taken me on holiday to another country.

The space on the right side of our pitch was empty until about a month in when a new caravan arrived. A single woman with a son.

My father introduced us. 'I'm Hector, and this is my lad, Gavin.'

The woman said her name was Kristina. The boy nodded from the door; he was called Abe, she told us. He was skinny with a healed broken nose and dark, curly hair. Our parents fell to talking. Abe's father had been a Coptic from Egypt, Kristina said, and he had chosen the name Abraam.

I was wary of the new boy. With the other children on the site, I had been able to reinvent myself. I had become a leader who could climb rock faces and head reconnaissance parties through the woods. I was no longer the boy who couldn't kick a football straight, who had cried when his schoolbag was set on fire during the first week of term. In the city, I'd been nervous of the dark, now it was like a second skin I could draw over my own.

'What's a Coptic?' I asked my father later.

He scratched his ear and frowned. 'People who have Christmas sometime in January,' he said.

I watched the boy over the next few days, coming and going, up and down the metal steps of their caravan. He made the first peace offering: a small bag of flavoured peanuts. 'We have tons of them,' he said. 'My mum works in the factory.' He said it like she still worked there, and he expected them to go back soon. The next day, I showed him the different pathways in the wood, and from then on we got along without effort.

At the centre of the idea behind the camp was a man in his fifties who lived in a long, horizontal-striped static van, parked up on bricks near the entrance. He called himself the frontrunner. He was the only one allowed a television, and it flickered violet through a side window late into the summer nights. As the weeks slid by, Abe and I sometimes stood outside and tried to see what show was on. Being away from television was the greatest hardship; I longed for it like some sweet, addictive food.

The date appointed for the end of the world was the last day in August. When we first arrived, the frontrunner had given speeches in the centre of the campground on a concrete patch where something with an industrial purpose might once have sat, a generator or septic tank. We were told that at the end, the pure – those on the caravan site as far as I knew – would rise up into the air like a flotilla of helium balloons and look down on the unsaved, who would have to struggle on through burning landscapes. I was raised by a mother entirely sceptical of religion, and at school, anything to do with God was treated with collective disdain by the kids, so these ideas seemed merely implausible to me. The frontrunner did not insist on the children listening to his homilies, and as the weeks wore on, he seemed to grow bored of delivering them, spending more time in his camper van.

The images themselves, however, found ways to seep into my mind. One night I woke gasping for air, and for a moment, I believed that the dark of the caravan was black smoke. I thrashed my arms and scratched at the underside of the bunk above me. After I escaped the cocoon of my sleeping bag, I had an urgent need to get up and away, to crack the caravan door open and suck in the cooler air of the awning.

'Close that door,' my dad said, but he didn't rise, so I stayed with my nose to the gap breathing deep like someone had attempted to smother me.

Other times I'd get that sharp drop feeling as I sifted between waking and sleep. I'd experience full seconds of falling through the sky, my powers of flotation lost because I was not pure enough. I'd jolt awake clinging to the mattress. It wasn't that I started to believe the end was coming but that the heat of adult conviction around me created an occasional feverishness.

These episodes only happened at night. The days were mostly full of light and exploration. We children had made the surrounding woods our territory. We played tig, hide and seek, cops and robbers, and dodgeball. New games were invented: mafia, zombies, hunters and big cats, where either side might kill the other, and Cold War. We didn't know exactly what the Cold War was, but Abe came out with the phrase, and we created a game where enemies could be frozen then shot. We collected tiny pebbles to use as bullets, hurling them at the unmoving target. If a child grew tearful, I stepped in and stopped it.

Sometimes me and Abe set out on our own. We were well matched, each just finished our first year of high school. We often played a question game centred around what was the worst thing. Boiled or drowned? Waking up as a slug or a midgie? Ears cut off or toes? Other times we'd start a small fire and melt things. I began to imagine Abe's mother and my father becoming a couple, though I rarely saw them speak.

With increasing frequency, I also ventured out alone at night, my dad deciding the surrounding area was safe enough. In those times, it was like the night itself was alive and on my side. I came back once with my knee pouring with blood. My dad saw it as I was about to get in the shower. 'Be more careful,' he said, returning to his reading material. The blood swirled away pink in the water. I didn't put a plaster on it and let a huge scab form.

In the week before the end was meant to come, an old man turned up solo in an unbelievably small caravan. My father called it an oil drum on wheels. The guy had brought so many books, he'd sit outside with them piled in high stacks like tall buildings, himself in a foldout deck chair, reading through one after the other. To us, he seemed to know a lot about science, history, politics, nature, because he'd speak about these subjects frequently. He was so sure the apocalypse was coming, it started us wondering and arguing.

On the evening before the date set for the end, Abe and I went exploring in the woods together. We didn't talk about it, instead we climbed trees, threw stones at targets. As we were heading back in the direction of the camp, we saw the frontrunner in a clearing with the older teenage girl. He was in one of the white shirts he always wore, and the girl was wearing a short yellow summer dress. We stopped and fell silent. They were talking at a slow, relaxed pace. The girl was leaning back against a tree, her chin tilted upwards, her butterfly tattoo showing. Next to her, the frontrunner looked ungainly – his thin, gangly limbs coupled with a belly that protruded like a pregnancy. We moved closer instinctively without giving each other any sign, scrambling behind a wild privet bush.

'You think you're smarter than me,' the frontrunner said.

'I'd only be gone for two days at the most.'

'There aren't going to be any more days.'

'But if there is, if it doesn't happen, I could just go and come straight back.'

'Are you listening to me? You're not to leave.'

'I won't speak to anyone.'

'You won't speak because you won't go anywhere.'

'I won't even think anything. I'll wipe my mind. I won't remember a thing until I'm back here and I see the caravans again.'

'You won't go in the first place.'

She looked down at her feet. Her tone changed, suddenly high and childlike. 'I don't like it when you choke me,' she said. I couldn't imagine what this meant. I could only think of choking as a way of trying to kill someone. Was she saying he'd tried to kill her?

He was quiet for a moment, then he said, 'You do like it.'

'Do the other things but don't do that, it feels as if I'm going to die.'

'You like it afterwards.'

'It feels like dying.' She straightened herself, squared her feet to him. 'Maybe I'll just leave. Maybe I'll tell the police—' She stopped abruptly as if the frontrunner had given her a look or sign. She stood staring up at him.

Without warning, without changing his position, he hit her with the flat of his palm. Her head bounded to the side. When she straightened, her nose was bleeding, a bright red square. He looked at her for a second and then slapped her again. The sharp clapping sound of it. I sucked in a breath. The girl did not speak but kept her wide eyes on him, her arms clamped by her side, like she would stand her ground.

I poked Abe's elbow, 'Shit, let's go.'

'Shouldn't we do something?'

'Like what? Let's go.'

We stepped backwards, trying not to make a sound. Our feet crunched on dry leaves, but the two figures seemed locked into place. At a few metres distance, we turned and ran. As we picked up speed, we tripped and scuffled over roots and rocks. We slowed when we reached the boundary of the woods, a point where we were still in shadow, and the campground was in light. The scent of barbecues, of burnt meat came drifting.

Abe and I turned to each other and stood for a moment. Eyes on each other. The summer air was buzzing, loaded with pine sap. Our faces were level. Instead of discussing what we'd witnessed, I leant forward and kissed him. Quick, wet, warm. I'd wanted to unsully us from what we'd seen, and kissing was the best thing I could think of. His lips pressed back for a heartbeat. I'd not expected that, and also, I had. We both pulled away. I clenched my fists, ran my tongue along the ridges inside my mouth. I waited for him to say something, but he did not, instead he tugged my T-shirt. I wasn't sure if he meant me to leave, or to take the T-shirt off. The faint crackle of footsteps came through the trees behind us. We ran. The frontrunner's voice called from the woods, 'Who's that there?'

We separated at our caravans and dashed to the doors. Once inside, I sat on the couch-bed breathless. My dad was not there. I froze in place, waiting for a sharp knock on the door. But none came. After a while, I retreated to my bunk and dozed in my sleeping bag, a familiar heat on my skin, more prickly than ever. I heard my dad return after I don't know how long, moving things quietly about the kitchen cupboards as if he was trying not to wake me.

In the morning, my dad and I rose late. The time for the end was sunset. My dad cooked the two of us a special breakfast of bacon, eggs, sliced tomatoes and mushrooms all heaped up on toast. We ate slowly, cutting the toast into square pieces. I understood that it was wrong to hit a woman but telling him about what I'd seen felt as unlikely as telling him about the kiss or asking if my mum had tried to contact us. After we finished eating, he spent that last afternoon teaching me how to play chess. I was a quick learner, or he made me feel that I was. I still remember repeating *knights go one, two and jump to the side*. It struck me as odd that he thought I'd need this knowledge if the world was about to expire.

As it grew closer to sunset, the whole population of the camp gathered outside, standing around the concrete circle. We looked loosely towards each other's faces, or at the sky or at the ground. The two babies were carried by their mothers in patterned slings. I was next to my father. Abe was next to me. The adults began to hold hands. So the children did too. By the stiff, half-hearted way they did it, I could tell that the gesture embarrassed most of the grown-ups as much as the kids.

'Thirty seconds,' the frontrunner said.

The time ticked down. I imagined what it would be like to rise into the sky, how my limbs would feel just hanging loose. Or if I didn't rise, what it would feel like to burn, skin sizzling. I thought of a time I'd got chilli pepper juice into a cut on my thumb, the intensity of pain on that millimetre of flesh.

'Hold steady, hold steady,' the man from the oil drum caravan called out. He had one of his big, old books under his arm.

'Fifteen seconds,'

I turned my eyes to the ground, Abe's hand loosely in mine, skin tickling.

Ten, nine, eight.

For the count down from ten, everyone joined in as if it was Hogmanay.

Five, four, three.

The moment came.

Silence.

The trees rustled.

I looked to the sky. Then down to about the level of people's knees.

I think I was the first one to see it. On the far side of the circle, a blurry, dark shape. My balance shifted. Something animal running towards us.

The chocolate spaniel. In the excitement of the last day, perhaps the door to his caravan hadn't been shut properly. The dog came hurtling into the circle, into our silence, and dashed around our legs. We waited. The spaniel weaved in and out as we stood firm. Carrying a pink rubber bone toy in his mouth, his tail thumped back and forth, hitting our shins, his gaze turned up to our faces. Wondering why no one responded to him. He went stitching between us as the end kept on not coming. The world refused to burn, and our bodies stayed rooted to the earth.

'Keep waiting,' the frontrunner said, his mouth barely seeming to open to speak the words.

'Hold steady,' said the oil drum man again, his eyes clenched shut. He was swaying slightly as if all his muscles were in tension with each other.

We waited. The dog slowed to a steadier pace, began sniffing round our feet. His tail-wagging stopped, as if we had bored him.

We kept waiting.

The children let their hands drop first. A woman – the spaniel's owner – began to giggle, raising her wrist to cover her mouth. My dad let go of my hand. Several more people started to laugh, high and nervous, and the teenage girl began to cry.

I knelt to the dog as it was going by and caught its silky head between my hands and ruffled its fur. Abe reached over and patted it. The other kids gathered round the dog, stroking it from all sides so that it dropped the toy and twisted right and left, grinning.

At last, the frontrunner took a breath and screamed at us children, 'Get out, get out, you little shites. Go on, go, you wee fuckers.'

So we ran, laughing, into our woodland, with the dog running in the middle of us.

We stayed in the woods a long time. We played games. Tig and hide and seek. Without anyone mentioning it, the more violent choices were excluded. Someone had somehow grabbed a packet of ready-made popcorn, which we shared until it spilled. Minor fights broke out, then calmed. Abe sat near me and handed round peanuts from his rucksack. A girl had brought a flashlight. As the darkness came on, we set the torch in the middle of our circle and sat and told jokes. Every bodily fluid was fitted into a punchline. At times we laughed so hard we couldn't breathe and repeatedly toppled over, rolled around.

Gradually, kids began to say they were cold. We ignored it at first, and then one of the younger boys stood and said, 'I'm going back.' So we all returned, separating out at the campground edge to go to our individual caravans.

'Bye,' Abe said to me as I moved off from him, and I shoved his shoulder jokingly, made him trip a little.

My dad was waiting for me. He was sitting on one of the couches; he had not made up the bed. He was drinking coffee from his plastic thermos cup.

'We're leaving,' he said.

'We won't wait until the morning?'

'Nope,' he said.

As we loaded everything into the car by torchlight, Abe and his mother stayed outside. They had a small fire going and did not make a move to pack. Over on the other side of the park, the frontrunner's television light was shivering. My dad and I finished filling the car, objects jammed into random spaces, all our litter in the boot. We were set to leave. I got into the passenger seat. As my dad started the engine, I waved to Abe, and he waved back, sitting crossed-legged on a deckchair by the fire. I never saw him again.

I remember the drive that night, the road seeming to stretch on forever, the lights of oncoming haulage vehicles pressing on my eyes between the patches of nodding sleep I took. As the morning light came, we arrived back in the driveway we had left all that time ago.

'You'll go back to school next week,' my dad said. I could say nothing in return.

I was slow walking through the iron school gates, my feet barely rising off the ground. I was bullied, again. But I found things were subtly changed between me and the other children in a way that was to remain.

My dad and I did not speak about the time at the caravan site in the years that followed. I went back to living with my mum and told her just the barest details, making it sound like a holiday park. It was only when I was in my twenties that I talked to my dad about it a little more. We were getting on well again by that time, after a few shaky years. I had a partner then, and my dad liked him.

One day, my dad and I were working on his old car in the garage, trying to figure out how to sort out the fuel filter without spending much money. Following a span of silence, he said, 'You know I am sorry about the episode with Breckinridge. He was a very convincing man.'

'I'm not sure I know who you mean?' I said.

'Breckinridge. The cult guy.'

'Oh shit. With the caravans? I don't think I ever knew his real name.'

'Yeah, that was the guy. He was very persuasive.' My dad flapped his hand. 'It's hard to explain now.'

'Why were you thinking of him?'

'He's in the news.'

I went upstairs to find the article online. The house had an old modem then, and it took a while, whirring and twanging. I found the piece eventually. The photograph loaded in slow strips. There was the man, his eyes pouched and tired, his hair sticking up in tufts. Convicted of three counts of assault and fraud, but the charges were from more recent times, only a year ago. He was sentenced to six years in prison. An electricity came into my jaw as I studied his face. I must have been more afraid of him than I realised at the time. I closed the browser down and sat with the hum of the monitor for a minute before heading back downstairs.

'Got bad after we left, apparently,' my dad said without looking round as I arrived at the garage door.

'How do you mean?'

'There was a lot of squabbling, as you can imagine. He claimed there was a new date. Then someone set fire to his caravan. Poured petrol all over it. He was in there and asleep. They had a hell of a time getting him out. Before that, one of the women had gone sort of nuts – they thought it might be her who lit the fire. She had shaved her head, some kind of protest, I don't know.'

'Which woman? The teenage girl, about nineteen?'

'I honestly don't know.'

'What happened after that?'

'I didn't hear much more, really. It was a long time back.'

'But the people next to us?' I said. 'Do you know anything about them? The boy, Abe?'

'Don't remember him?'

'With his mum. The caravan right by us. Kristina, I think her name was.'

'Oh yeah.' My dad gave a huff of a laugh. 'She was a handful alright. We had a bit of a – well, never mind. No, I didn't hear anything about what happened to them.'

I looked at the tools spread out on the garage floor. 'The leader guy is going to prison by the sound of it.'

My dad nodded. 'I am sorry about it, taking you off to that place, with those people.'

'It was a long time ago,' I said. 'And I got something from it, in my own way.' We carried on with the car. He didn't try to get me to name whatever it was I'd got, and that was fine with me because I preferred not to have to pin it down.

'Very persuasive,' he repeated after a time. 'And then it all collapsed up in a moment. Like turning on a light switch in a dark room and finding you've been in the wrong house all along.'

When I picture what went on after we left, I see the static van burning on the grass like a torch and the older teenage girl running into the woods, petrol on her jeans. Abe and the other children run, too, the dog among them. The girl is fierce with her newly shaved scalp, punching the night air. And after he's dragged out coughing and gagging, after he's more or less regained composure, the frontrunner gets in his car, a tail-folded peacock, and he leaves. He doesn't do anything else; he doesn't try to reassert his authority in any way. He doesn't even pack up. He just drives off down the forest road. That's how I choose to see it end.

Owlets

Chicks

We had planned to paint the barn blue and call it a library. We couldn't find the key that first evening, so it was only on the second day that we discovered the nest. Above the central cross-beam, a thicket of pellets and feathers with two owlets in the centre, their faces like dandelions gone to seed. 'Well, that's that out the window,' Jack said. I could not disagree; we couldn't disrupt them.

They were enchanting, like small supernatural beings. I'd think about them at night, the two pale spectres in the dark of the barn, there all the time, awake while we slept. The impossibility of knowing what it was like to be them. What did they sense, feel, see? What did they think, even, if such a term could be applied to them?

Jack had a friend of his from a wildlife society come and tag and weigh them. I watched them being lifted from their nest-world by gloved hands, their beaks open in pink outrage. 'There are superstitions about owls, aren't there?' I said to him.

'Yeah, barn owls predict a death in the household.' We both laughed in a nervy sort of way.

It was about two weeks after that when we heard about the missing girl. It was actually on the television news. Jack and I offered to be in a search party, but the police didn't want that kind of thing so early on. Perhaps you can see where this is going. I am certain I checked the barn properly on that first day, I searched all the corners, lifted up old machinery she couldn't possibly be under. The place was empty. But come the following night, when I set out to look at the owlets, there she was, sitting in the corner of the barn, the hood of her coat pulled down so it hung over her eyes. She was holding one of the baby owls. How she had got it out of the nest, I do not know. There was no ladder. But there she sat, cradling it in her arms, the little thing hissing like a cat. The other in the nest looking on, watching the whole scene. There is a saying that an owl has *more the face of a Christian than a bird,* and the one in the nest did have the look of a painted saint, peering down at the girl.

'What have you got there?' I said.

She didn't respond. I took a step towards her. She kept her head down. What was I going to do? I couldn't snatch the owl from her, it might get injured. The little thing still hissing away at me.

'Please, would you give the chick to me? They're delicate, they're awfully delicate. We wouldn't want it to get hurt, and its mother will worry.'

She mumbled something. I couldn't make it out.

'Please, give the owl to me.' I took another step towards her. She muttered something again. 'I can't hear what you're saying.'

I knelt close to her.

'Don't phone the police,' she said.

'Ah, I know, I know, but I'm probably going to have to because everyone's been looking for you, and we could get into trouble if we don't.'

She mumbled something else.

'What are you saying, dear?' I was not in the habit of calling people dear. I shuffled closer on my knees.

'I'll wring its neck,' she whispered.

I leant back.

'What?'

'You call the police, I'll snap its neck like it's a hen.' I stood up and stepped away from her. I couldn't help projecting fear onto the owlet watching from the nest. I found myself imagining it wanted its sibling back. But of course, owls sometimes eat their siblings. They are not sentimental that way.

'For God's sake, just give me the chick.'

'You call the police, I'll snap it,' she said.

I stepped backwards towards the barn door. 'You little witch,' I said. 'You just dare. I'll snap your neck.'

I hurried back into the house and phoned the police. I couldn't keep still, pacing the kitchen. They came out within fifteen minutes. A male and female officer. Two tall figures. I could hardly watch as they strode through the barn door.

But the chick was alright. She had not damaged it.

Jack followed the officers into the barn with a ladder and saw that the owlet was returned to the nest.

The girl was taken away, wrapped in a tartan blanket from our bedroom. Jack had brought it down thinking she looked cold. I would have preferred that he had asked me first. I watched from the kitchen, without the lights on. I didn't think she'd be able to see me as she got in the car, but she did seem to cast a look in my direction.

When she was gone, I headed back to the barn to see the two chicks in the nest. 'Right as rain,' Jack said. They both looked at me with faces like Venetian masks, and I couldn't tell which one of them had been out of the nest.

The fact that the girl had been found was mentioned briefly on the regional news. The local paper ran a headline the next day, *Our Caitlyn Found Safe*. No more was said of her after that, nothing in the paper, nothing on the television.

We didn't know why she had run away, why does a girl that age not want to go home? I was left with a sense that I'd carried out a small act of betrayal. I'd called her a witch, though she was just a child. There is another superstition that owls are witches in disguise. Maybe that was at the back of my mind. Over time I've come to think I handled it as well as anyone could. I saw her once in the town, wearing the same hooded jacket though the sun was out. She did not look at me and perhaps wouldn't even have recognised me if she had. We often believe others think of us more than they do. We've got to know a few local people now. Surely we'd have heard, if there was something further to her story.

So, summer came around, and the owlets fledged. Another friend of Jack's, a photographer, visited and took some beautiful pictures of them in flight. We hung three enlarged black and white prints on the wall leading up the stairs. We're hoping the owls will have another brood this coming spring. We've rather given up on our library. I do not fear the ill omen barn owls are supposed to offer; I like to think if anything, they'll bring us luck.

Air Gun

Caitlyn settles in the space she has made for watching, nestled down deep by the trunk of the rowan. Over time, she has worn her own path to the house, through the ferns. Tonight the woman and the man are at home. They are eating in the dining room, placed opposite each other at the table, the window lit like the windows of the pretend, plaster buildings in the folk museum. From this distance, their movements remind her of the motion of the museum's mechanical dolls, leaning forward or back, their arms raising with a glass or loaded fork. Their mouths open and close, telling nothing. All the time she watches, her air pistol rests snug against her back pocket, sitting in the holster she made for herself in home economics. It hangs from her belt under her coat and gives her a feeling of being a cowgirl.

Since the time last year when she first found the place, when the police were called out, she has been visiting the house in secret, making her own route that loops down into the valley and up again instead of using the road. To hold a baby owl is like clutching a goblin – she would like to do it again. But the barn doors are shut fast now with a fist of a padlock and a gleaming chain.

What they've not done, though, is padlock the house. The back door has only one deadlatch cylinder lock, and the spare key for it is kept under a stone frog on the third step.

Caitlyn has taken to visiting the house when they are out, letting herself in, pretending it is her own home, that she lives there by herself and never has to go back anywhere else. In the bedroom, she likes to put on the woman's lipstick, wild pink colours that make the inky patches under her eyes stand out darker. The top drawer of the dresser is full of underwear made of slippery material. In the kitchen, there is always an open bottle of something sweet, port or sherry or orange liqueur, and she likes to drizzle two fingers' worth into a teacup. She'll sip her drink slowly, striding about the hyacinth-scented living room, running her fingers over the pristine furniture. Licking the stickiness from her lips. Sashaying. When she has finished drinking, she always rinses the cup out with lemon liquid and leaves it back on the dish rack, untouched.

Tonight, the couple are in, so there is no visiting the house. The wind is up, vexing, and she is cold already, crouched by the rowan tree. She may pick up ticks and have to pluck them out later, obese full stops that will cling to her ankles and midriff. But the rain has stayed off. A white owl swoops and flies into the barn through an opening near the roof. She pulls out her air gun and dusts it with the sleeve of her coat.

Readjusting her position in the ferns, she takes aim at the window of the dining room, first at one bright face, then at the other. If she assassinates one of them, gets a good clean shot to the forehead, she will take their place. The house will be hers, and so will the bulky car, and the shining bottles of nectar drinks, and the barn where the owls live. She will never have to go back, and the oil-coloured bruises on her thighs and biceps will vanish permanently, exchanged for clear, unblotted skin.

She stands up, exposed, and straightens her arms out in front of her, both hands clasping the gun, posing like a hitman in a film. The faces in the window turn towards her.

There is a second where all gazes meet, and then without naming her intention to herself, she pulls the trigger. Her eyelids squeeze shut at the same moment, and there is a bang and a scream and the sound of cracking glass.

She opens her eyes and finds a white spiderweb of lines has appeared in the middle of the lit window, and the two faces are still looking at her. She'd thought the pane would shatter and fall like a sheet of ice, but she has not broken through the glass at all, and the faces behind it remain intact.

They stare at her for a moment and then they are moving from the dining room, the hall light is on, and then the back door is open, and she can hear the woman shouting, 'You witch, you little witch.'

She runs down through the ferns, into the slope of the valley. She moves blindly, trusting the ground not to break her ankles. She thunders into the woods, evening-birds flapping out of her way. She keeps speeding on, her heart and her feet beating at the same pace. The wind billows and sinks and rises again, the trees hiss and shake. As she gets deeper into the wood, she grins and keeps going, and she knows that the woman is right, she is a witch, and she is making the trees bend and snap to her own will. The whole wood bows and trembles to her power.

Bad Blood

The ground was solid with frost. Small, frozen raindrops decorated the tree branches. Walking out to the barn in the morning, a dream filtered back to him in flashes and starts. He'd dreamt that he was an owl. He'd sat up on the high beam where they'd normally roost, and he'd watched his human wife come and go below him. He knew somehow she was looking for him. *She won't find me here*, he'd thought, not with any malice, but with mild curiosity to see if she would look up and spy his owl form. She never did.

He couldn't recall ever having been anything other than himself in a dream. Entering the barn now, he rubbed at his forehead. There was something disturbing about losing his human shape and, in the dream, not minding. He'd tell Charlotte, and she'd find it funny; that would burst the skin of it.

In wintertime, the owls used the barn for roosting though they had no chicks to feed. He looked up towards the roof. The owls' beam was bare except for hardened droppings. With the cold well set in, they were often still hunting in daylight hours. They'd be out there among the fields, scanning from resting posts for minuscule movements and sounds, scuttlings and scrimmagings.

He set up his wood bench. With some experimentation, he had learned he could work in the barn without scaring the owls as long as he moved smoothly. He fixed a piece of wood into the vice and began sawing. The back and forth rhythm of the blade, the flow of the dust created a kind of trance. After a time, he heard the crackle of a car pulling up on the gravel outside. He put the saw down and stepped to the doorway, his breath clouding the air. It was their two-fields-away neighbour, who owned the fishmongers in the town centre. The window of the car wound down.

'Morning.'

'Morning. Thought you'd want to know,' the neighbour said. 'They're looking for the girl again.'

'Oh, are they?'

'Imagine the police will be round here.'

'I'll keep an eye out.'

'She's really done something this time.' The neighbour leant his elbow out of the window.

'How so?'

'Something crazy.' He looked pleased, to have this to tell, like he was talking of his own heroics.

'Oh?'

'She's gone and stuck a knife in her stepfather.'

'Christ. Is he—?'

'No, he's in hospital. A penknife, in the leg.'

'What could've possessed her?'

'Some daft argument, people are saying. Lucky, missed the artery.'

'She's a wild girl.'

'Yeah. You know the older brother is in prison for possession of stolen goods?' The neighbour leant further, his breath puffing, steam from a train.

'I didn't know.'

'Sometimes I wonder. Same family. I wonder if there really is such a thing as bad blood. You know what I mean?'

He gave a small nod, only meaning he did know the phrase. He looked around at the gleaming frost. 'It's colder today.'

'Aye, it is. Anyway, keep a lookout. She might come hiding.' The window wound up. He watched the car pull away.

He told Charlotte over lunch. 'They'll be worried about her, out in the cold,' she said, tearing apart her bread and dipping it. Her animosity to the girl had cooled in the time since the cracked window.

'She'll be alright,' he said.

'How do you know?' She looked over her soup, her sharpening gaze.

'I suppose I don't.'

He didn't tell her about the owl dream. It seemed only silly now.

Later, when he was doing the dishes, two police officers stopped by. They wanted him to open up the barn. He showed them in. They shone torch beams into the corners, picked up the boards he was going to use for the shelves, looked behind the touring bikes they'd bought. One of the owls was roosting, settled down in its spot, claws gripping the rafter. It watched them with eyes minimally open, two fragments of coal in snow.

The police completed their search, tramped back to their car. 'If you notice anything, let us know.'

He heard no more about it that day. At night, the security light they'd fitted clicked on and off. Click, nothing there. Click, neighbour's cat. Click, a small, tawny vixen who always appeared at the same time. Click, nothing again. When this happened, he got the urge to search around the room he stood in. He had a sense there was a little wild animal inside the house, invisible.

The next morning, while he was reading the newspaper in the kitchen, he saw the neighbour's car pull up in the driveway. The sound of the door slam ringing in the chilled air.

'Guessed you'd want to hear.'

'What's this now?'

'They found her. The girl. She was in the shell of the mill.'

'Was she OK?'

'Fit as a fiddle.'

'Glad she didn't come here,' he said, glancing back at the barn. 'And that she's alright.'

'Police found her huddling with a makeshift fire. A near thing she didn't freeze to death. She'll be charged, I imagine – grievous bodily harm or that. She'd thrown the knife away, and her shoes. But the daft thing was the clothes she had on were all spattered in blood anyway.'

'Not exactly a master criminal.'

'No. She left with the police quiet as you like. I spoke to Joan about it.' The female officer who the neighbour was friendly with.

'That's that over then.'

'Makes you wonder, though,' the neighbour said, one eye narrowing. 'Like I said. Bad blood.' The window wound up.

In the afternoon, he worked in the barn again. The quietness was so deep, it seemed to slow time. As he was taking up a new piece of wood, his eye caught something on the barn floor. A couple of glints in the far corner, among the sawdust. He took a step towards the shine. There were three things; a crisp packet, a crumpled soft drink can, a penknife wiped clean. She had been here then, after the police. In the night or early morning, on her way to the mill, somehow she had got in. But he had locked the door. The padlock, he had undone it today to get in. Had she picked it and then carefully closed it up again? He looked around him. There was no other way. The owls came and went through a small circle of stone where a window had been once, high up. No reaching that. She'd not even tried to hide the objects themselves. They looked like the remains of a modern-day spell. Cautiously, he took a cloth from the bench and wrapped the litter and the knife without touching any of it. He took a few steps round in a circle, wondering what to do. The police would need to be informed. It dawned on him he shouldn't have picked them up. Weren't they, in a pathetic way, part of a crime scene? He laid the parcel on the barn floor and wandered over to the house to phone.

The evidence was collected, the police saying mildly that he ought not to have moved it. But they told him no charges had been pressed against the girl. Her stepfather perhaps just wanting her home. Relieved the objects were gone, he returned to the barn to simply look, as he often did.

Both owls were there, eyes closed, heads tucked forward as if in prayer. Resting from their hard winter life. He'd buy a new lock, to keep them safe. He wasn't concerned about any possessions in the barn, only about them. They had enriched his day-to-day world with an uncanny presence, and he worried for them in the harshness of winter. But these two were crafty; they would have learned their territory, the best hunting grounds, and that would serve them well in the cold nights which offered little prey. A dab of luck, and the two owls would survive and flourish, ready to be parents again come spring.

Nightjar

You told me winter didn't begin until December twenty-first in astronomical terms. I rejected this: it was winter now. Just gone six o'clock and the world so dark the road in front of us seemed to emerge from nowhere, to be created in the span of the headlights a few metres at a time.

'It's definitely this road?' I said.

'Where else could it be?' You'd taken a wrong turn twice already.

The landscape to either side was a blank. The road carried on rolling itself out, offering up sudden twists and the occasional startled sheep resting on the tarmac. Nothing upon nothing beyond the road. Until, after a good span of time and way up ahead, tiny lights appeared winking through trees. I focused, sat forward in the passenger seat. They looked like fairy lights, several strings of them in a haphazard arrangement.

'That must be the house,' you said. 'I knew it was down here.'

'You should know. You've been enough times.'

'In the daylight. Not at night on these shitty wee roads.'

The strings of light seemed to change shape as they were hidden or revealed by dark objects passing the car. 'I didn't take your wife's family as the type for fairy lights – you said they're cynical about Christmas.'

'People can be surprising.' Your wife had arrived at her parents' house earlier in the week, she was waiting for us there.

We turned a wide corner, and I could tell somehow that the sea was directly to our left, though nothing was visible. I could feel the waves far below, down a cliff edge. Perhaps I could hear them underneath my conscious hearing. The fairy lights now were in front of us, and they had fixed their shape in an arch so that it looked as if they'd been looped over the roof. The side of the building facing us seemed to have no windows, or no windows were lit.

Your wife had invited me to stay. We'd been talking about her parents' home in the west highlands, and I said *sounds like heaven, the mountains by the sea*, and she said *come up sometime, we'll all go*. Months later, the three of us in a bar, and she mentioned she was heading to her parents' for a week, and you were going for the weekend only because of work. And I said, brazenly, *remember I was to go sometime?* And your wife said, *oh yeah, you bring her, why not? We'll make a wee weekend of it.*

The car nosed down a steep hill and then up again. A bird burst out of the undergrowth and shot across the front windscreen. A mottled fawn blur briefly lit by the headlights.

'What was that?'

'Looked sort of like a pheasant,' I said. 'But not quite. I don't know. We missed it anyway.'

As we drew closer to the lights, the warmth in the car became dense. I rolled the window down a half inch. 'Turn the heater off for a bit.' The outside air tasted of bog myrtle and darkness, I thought. I knew the darkness had no flavour, but I was trying to be poetic even inside my own head. It was only once we had taken a right off the main road and were a dozen metres or so from the lights that we could make out that there was no house. The lights had been strung up over a copse of trees.

'That's weird,' I said. You stopped the car and said nothing. The tiny lights shimmered in front of us. 'Who put them there?' We sat still, watching them dance in the wind. A prickling on my palms. Turning, I said, 'Was it you?'

You faced me, twisting in your seatbelt, eyes on my eyes for a moment, and I felt like I had slipped backwards to a younger self. 'Might have been fairies,' you said, small smile.

'That's not helpful.' I swiped at your shoulder. 'I want to get a closer look.'

We got out of the car and walked towards the lights. 'Someone put them here,' I said. 'I'm guessing it's a sort of practical joke. If it wasn't you.' I glanced at your face. The white light made your skin appear as if lit by a fairy tale moon. Together we walked under the arch. There is something hypnotic about tiny lights in the dark, something that seems to transform the world slightly. There was no additional illumination so that, in front of us, there might have been miles of woodland or just a field's worth of trees.

We began walking along a tractor path between the trunks, thick mud with the texture of buttercream under our boots. It felt good to stretch our legs. Round a bend, an unnatural gleam appeared. A car, someone was parked on the rutted track. 'Maybe it's the person who set up the fairy lights,' I said. Just as we drew near to the bonnet, I jolted back. A figure, a face forming. A man stood to the left of the driver's door in a dark jacket.

'Jesus God,' you said.

'Jesus, you gave me a fright,' I said, instinctively making my voice jovial, non-threatening.

The man stepped towards us before he spoke. Looking back, that felt like a small power play. 'You haven't seen a wee boy?' he said.

'No.'

'No one.'

'Are you from here?' the man asked.

'No, just visiting family,' you said. *Not my family*, I could have said.

'I'm the gamekeeper on the estate. I'm looking for my son. He's eight years old.'

My eyes adapting now, added more detail to his face. He had a wide chin and deep grooves under his eyes. He seemed old to have an eight-year-old son. A late-life romance, I guessed.

'We'll help you look. You lost him just round here?' you said.

'He ran off from the car.'

'How big are these woods?'

'Not big, just a few trees. He'll be here somewhere. He knows this place.' His voice was completely level.

You switched on your phone torch. The dark became darker outside the circle of light. Beyond the car, the track split into two smaller footpaths going off in two directions. 'We could walk round the other way from you, see if we can find him,' I said.

'Aye, do that.'

'What's his name?'

'Ben.'

The two of us headed along the path in the opposite direction to the man, calling out the boy's name. Once we were far enough away, you whispered in my ear, 'He might be a nutter. A serial killer.' Your breath on my ear like a butterfly's wings. Once, in your flat on a spring morning, a red admiral flew in the window and landed on my elbow. We'd been having breakfast together, we'd had an argument, and the butterfly made us both laugh.

'It's all fun and games until one of us gets shot,' I said.

'He had a gun,' you said.

'What? Not really?'

'Well, he's a gamekeeper.'

'But did you see it?'

'I saw it. Didn't you? I saw it glinting under his arm. The way they always carry guns.'

'Shit.'

'I'll protect you,' you said, taking my arm, a mock-protective gesture.

'It might be you he shoots. We shouldn't joke. The guy's kid is missing.'

'Or he made that up to lure us into the trees.'

'Don't,' I said. 'Poor guy. This is freaking me out.'

Once, you and I had been lovers. I mean one time only. It was the week I'd had a health scare and it had all turned out fine, but I was rattled by it. We were at my flat, and we'd curled up together in your sleigh bed like forest animals. It had been a stormy night, I swear. I'm not just romanticising. The wind had howled around us, and I'd woken and slept and woken and slept. We weren't drunk, it had happened sweetly and naturally, and then it had not happened again.

But, the night with the fairy lights. It was cold, and the track seemed to go on and on. I regretted leaving my gloves and scarf in the car. I was just about to suggest we turn back when I saw a movement up ahead, a flash of white between the trees.

'Ben!' I called. 'I saw him – Ben! – I think it was him, running over there.'

'Ben!' you shouted. 'We'll probably scare him, he doesn't know who the hell we are.'

I stared into the trees. I could see nothing. I couldn't think of anything else it might have been; there'd be no white animals here, except maybe a stray sheep. But the movement of what I'd seen, it had to be a little person running upright, the height of a child.

'I'm sure it was him.'

'Shh,' you said.

'Shh what?' I could just see your face in the dark.

'Shh, I want to see if I can hear him.'

We both stood still. I heard the wind through the trees, the crepe paper rustle of the leaf bed. Nothing else. 'Let's go back and tell the guy we've seen him. The kid's not going to run up to strangers,' I said.

So we did an about-turn. We retraced our steps. But as we followed the path back, we came to a fork. I hadn't noticed any forks on the way out; we'd just walked straight ahead. I guess the fork had been pointing behind us on the way out, so it was less obvious.

'This one, I think, it looks more like the main path,' I said.

'OK.' You strode out in front. The torch made the branches near us flicker and judder with each step. Another fork appeared.

'Damn it,' I said.

You pointed. 'This bit seems more like the main path.'

'They look pretty similar.'

'We've got to pick one.'

'Alright then.' We took the left fork, though both tracks were narrow and overgrown. I followed behind you.

Smack.

A branch hit me in the eye. Not right in the eye but on the eyelid. Instinct had made me blink, though I had no awareness of it coming. I yelled and covered my face with my hand.

'What? What?' Your voice angry.

'I got hit in the eye. A branch. It just gave me a fright.'

'You're OK?'

'I'm fine.' You put your hand up to the hand of mine that was covering the eye. Gently you prised my fingers away, shone the torch on my face.

'It looks alright.'

'That's what I said. I was just startled.'

'Be more careful.'

It seemed we'd already been trying to walk back longer than it took us to walk out. My feet started to ache, and there was no glimpse of the fairy lights. I kept stepping in puddles, and water had soaked through the fabric of my trainers. I could feel mud getting in somehow, a graininess between my toes. You stopped and listened again.

'What is it?'

I listened too. There was a faint metallic sound, like the wide blade of a saw being flexed. A word flashed into my mind.

'Nightjar.'

'What?'

'It's a nightjar, the bird.'

We fell silent. The noise came again.

'It doesn't sound like a birdcall,' you said.

'That's the thing – they don't sound like birds. They make this weird noise. That must be what we saw on the road. I had a feeling I knew what it was.'

'Why do they call them nightjars?'

'I don't know.' The name made me picture a row of black jars in a lit room, holding pieces of night-time. We stood still and listened until the noise stopped.

'I think we're lost,' you said.

'Should we turn round again?' Before you could answer, we heard the gunshot.

Years ago now, one night, I fell asleep on your couch, but we did not have sex. I woke, and you were asleep in your bed, and I stood at the door to your bedroom and just watched you. After a minute or so, I grew afraid you would wake to see me watching, so I went through to the kitchen and ate some cherry tomatoes straight from the fridge, bursting cold on my teeth. In the morning, over cereal, you told me you were getting married, and I said I was happy for you.

So the gunshot rang out. We froze, hands on each other's arms, and then we both started giggling. It seemed funny for a few split seconds, even as my heart was jammering in my neck. We stopped laughing and kept holding each other.

'Do you think he's killed someone?' you said. The laughter was still in your voice.

'Yes,' I said, breaking out with giggling again. I felt sick. 'But really, what the fuck?'

'It could be anything, right? He's a gamekeeper, maybe he saw a... I don't know, whatever gamekeepers shoot round here.'

'What would he shoot, it's pitch dark?'

'A nightjar?' you said.

'I think they're protected.'

'Maybe it was a warning shot.'

'A warning to a nightjar?'

'Maybe,' you said.

We decided we were not on the right path; this one was becoming far too cluttered and boggy. We agreed to retrace our steps. I kept flinching away from branches, somehow still gathering scratches on my arms and face. Because we had reversed, I was leading, using the light from your phone. When I saw the track split into a fork again, I guessed the route we should take, and neither of us commented on it. My face was becoming numb with cold, the scratches felt like thread-thin burns.

A year after you got married, your wife had a miscarriage. You were away on a work trip; it happened on the Monday, and you were travelling back on the Tuesday, so I came round in the evening and made her cups of peppermint tea. We sat on your sofa and watched old episodes of M.A.S.H and didn't speak. She was still wearing her green nurse's uniform under a cardigan. Whenever I attempted to talk to her, she'd wave a hand so I knew not to try. She wouldn't let me close the curtains after dark. We sat on the couch in the huge bay window of your old flat with all that darkness behind us. I think of it now alongside the word nightjar. Two silent creatures in a lit jar, with the night outside and pressing at the glass.

Finally, I saw the fairy lights through the branches. Like a mirage at first, they blinked and shivered far up ahead. The path led us back to them from a different angle. As I walked, I was waiting for the man to reappear. I had a twitchy sense that he would jump out on us. My throat was holding in a high-pitched noise. We reached the arch of the lights and I could see the torch beam bouncing off your car.

'Made it,' I whispered. I realised I hadn't seen the man's car. 'Where is he?'

We shone the torch around. The tree trunks whorled with old faces. He was not there, and his car was gone.

'Should we look for him? Tell him we saw the boy?' you said.

'If he's gone, he must have picked up the boy. He wouldn't leave without him, would he? Surely your wife's folks will know who he is?' My breath was coming in small pants like I had been running.

'Did we see the boy, though?'

'I think I saw him. He must have him if he's gone now.' I tugged at your sleeve. 'I don't want to get killed, please let's just go.'

'You're right, you're right. Let's leave.' We folded into the car. I had the sense that something would happen. Someone would rip the door open, drag us out. You put the key in the ignition. The car started up. We reversed away from the fairy lights, and my body eased into my seat, and we were back onto the road. As the car was picking up speed along the main track, relief fell on me like a sack of feathers emptied over my head.

We hurtled onwards. I was tempted to lean against your shoulder, but I did not. 'I thought you put the lights there for me,' I said

'Don't make me sad,' you said.

We arrived at your in-laws' house. Your wife was there. She enfolded you like light from a star, then hugged me, kissed me. That woman with her little bird hands and her throaty laugh, her absurd array of talents. No one could not have loved her. We were late, but your parents-in-law had kept cold chicken pie and potatoes for us.

As we ate, the three of them hovered round the table like anxious waiters. Your wife brought us salt, pepper, paper napkins. We told them about the gamekeeper. 'There is no gamekeeper round here,' your father-in-law said.

'No kids that age either. We know all the local children. They're either tiny-wee, or grown,' your mother-in-law said.

We wondered if we should phone the police. Had there been a child? If so, was it really the man's son, or had something else been going on? In the end, we did phone the police. We didn't want to be those people who didn't do anything. The man's voice at the other end of the phone gave us an incident number. He said a police officer would phone us back.

We talked late around the kitchen table, just the three of us, gripping giant glasses of wine, your wife's parents gone to bed. 'We maybe saw a nightjar on the drive up,' I said.

'Could have been, they are round here,' your wife said. 'You know people used to believe they stole milk from goats? Of course, it's not true, but it's kind of a cool idea, isn't it? This bird that turns up at night and steals something so intimate from a sleeping animal.'

Two hours later, at a quarter to midnight, a policewoman called. I described everything again, as I had the first time. She told me there was no evidence a crime had been committed, so there would be no further action. Her voice, crackling towards me, was placid, perhaps faintly sarcastic. Still, she said, they'd create a file in case anything related came through.

Maybe the man was just messing around, your wife suggested. Perhaps it was his child, but he was joking about being a gamekeeper. Or perhaps there wasn't a child, and that was the joke. I nodded and thought maybe the white thing I saw was a ghost or someone's blown-away laundry. 'You know, it could have been Dougie, up to his tricks. He lives down the road. He does things a bit like this,' she said.

'Does he have a gun?' I asked.

'He might do. I think he goes deer stalking sometimes.'

In the morning, the three of us drove back to the location of the fairy lights. The sun shone through the clouds, the lights were switched off, and we could see where they were twist-tied to the trees. 'I wouldn't have gone into the woods in the dark in the first place, I'm not as brave as you two,' your wife said.

She wandered to the trees now, to try to see how the lights were set up.

'It wasn't you then?' I said in a low voice.

'What wasn't me?'

'The lights.'

'How could it be? We drove up together,' you said.

We joined your wife. She'd found where the lights were connected, a black cable leading to a car battery. We didn't stick around long. I still had a sense that something was about to happen in that place, and I wanted to get away.

I watched the local news. No stories about missing children. We never got to meet this Dougie and so could not confirm or deny if it was him, *up to his tricks*.

On the last evening, the three of us stepped outside in the dark with warm mugs of tea and tasted the frost in the air. There were no fairy lights in sight, though far in the distance, we could see the warning red of a lighthouse winking. A great rift in the clouds revealed stars as plentiful as a countertop sugar spill. A planet, Jupiter you thought, stood out above us like a flake of ice.

'Winter nights,' your wife said, smiling.

'Almost,' you said. 'Not yet. We've all that still to come.'

And that was it, that was our weekend together. We went to bed, and headed back in two cars the next morning through bright winter sun. Years later, after your wife died, I stayed around, I tried to be there for you, but it was not me you chose.

Black and Orange Caterpillars

The morning Ailsa was due to start working at the café, the road leading out from the village was covered in black and orange caterpillars. In places, she had to walk on her tip-toes. Some of them were as small as catkins, others as thick as men's fingers. Whenever she saw a car coming, she tried to gather a few onto a leaf and carry them to the verge. The smallest seemed the most helpless, so she collected these first.

She arrived at the café fifteen minutes late. Mrs Graham, who ran and owned the place, told her off in front of the cook and the kitchen assistant. While Mrs Graham spoke, Ailsa watched the shoal of fish that the sun created on the floor as it shone through the ivy crowded window. Two weeks ago, she'd gone out on a trout fishing trip with her dad, and on the way back, they'd stopped at the café for milkshakes, and Mrs Graham had written their order down and smiled and nodded and shuffled off. Now she was Ailsa's boss.

She gave Ailsa a mint green apron and showed her how to work the coffee machine. Ailsa stared at the back of her head. She had long grey hair in a plait that hung between her shoulders. Although she was not youthful, she looked too young for grey hair.

The kitchen assistant was a boy from another village. Ailsa recognised him from the shop where he had worked last summer but didn't know his name. He was short with waxy, dark hair, and he wore a T-shirt with printed shapes on it that looked like an inkblot test. The cook was Polish, tall and broad. He lived just out beyond Ailsa's village with his Scottish wife and three identical black labradors.

The first customers arrived at nine o'clock. A woman and a man with a fat-cheeked baby boy. They were from Birmingham, staying at the campsite out on the cliff edge. The woman held the little boy on her lap; he was dressed in a bear-cub hood, and he clasped at the air between them as Ailsa took their order.

'Are you from round here then, love?'

'Yeah,' Ailsa said.

'You've always lived here?'

'Yup.'

'Lucky you, it's so beautiful. I was just saying – wasn't I? – I could happily spend my whole life here.' Ailsa smiled back at the woman.

She had other, similar conversations that morning, the customers each telling her how lucky she was. She thought about the caterpillars as she worked. It bothered her that they might feel pain as the cars hit them. She harboured a wavering belief in reincarnation. It was possible she would be a caterpillar one day. She'd wondered about telling the customers to watch out for them, but Mrs Graham was usually nearby, observing and smiling, so she said nothing. Mrs Graham's smiles seemed to cost her something.

Ailsa was allowed to take a quick lunch late in the day while Mrs Graham served the customers. She ate her jam sandwiches in the kitchen. The Polish cook, whose name was

Mateusz, stood over the hob and asked after her parents and if it was her last year of school and what was she going to do when she left? She said they were well, and she was just about to begin her last year and she didn't know. She did not speak to the kitchen assistant, and he didn't look at her, eating his small lunch of pasta from a plastic box at the other end of the folding table. His name was Ewan, Mrs Graham had told her; he'd made no attempt to introduce himself.

They were allowed to have a styrofoam cup of coffee from the machine with their lunch, and so Ailsa made herself one, never having tried coffee before. She carefully tore and tipped three packets of brown sugar into it.

'Three sugars, huh?' said Mateusz.

'What?'

'Nothing at all.'

It tasted bitter even with the sugars, and scalded the roof of her mouth. For the rest of the day, she could feel her own heartbeat.

At closing time, Mrs Graham stood at the door to take her apron back. 'Be on time tomorrow, mmm?' she said with a flick of a smile.

Outside, it was raining, and most of the caterpillars were gone. Ailsa kept her head up so she couldn't see the squashed ones. Or the live ones. She didn't want to stop to rescue them. When she arrived home, she stretched out on her bed and took her socks off and read a bashed copy of *A Midsummer Night's Dream* because they were going to be studying it next term. She could only follow it in small pieces, some sections shimmering with meaning, others opaque.

She worked Saturdays and Sundays, which had the effect of reversing the week, making the weekdays bright and the weekends dull. On the morning of the second Saturday, she dropped a tray of macaroni cheese in front of a family with children her own age who watched her with sarcastic eyes.

'Right,' said Mrs Graham, 'let's get this cleared up, shall we?' Ailsa's face felt scorched, she could never help the blood rising when anyone stared.

At lunch, she sat directly across from the kitchen assistant but did not speak to him. The cook was chopping a large gathering of vegetables to make up a second batch of the soup of the day. She'd seen him nibbling on carrot sticks or cured meats at times, but Mrs Graham didn't seem to take a lunch or snack. If she ate, it was in secret.

As Ailsa was scrunching away her tinfoil package, Mrs Graham brushed past her back to put something on a shelf. 'What on earth is that on your fingers?' Ailsa looked down at her own hands, but she couldn't see anything except a few smudges. She looked across at the boy's hands. On each of his fingernails were splodges of black nail polish, chipped into shapes that resembled tiny countries. 'Never again, OK? You can wear what you want in your own time, but I've got to have some standards here.'

The boy said nothing, but when Mrs Graham was gone, he caught Ailsa's eye and shook with silent laughter.

On Thursday, Ailsa walked down to the lochside with Jill from school. They sat with their legs over the edge of a rock, the water halfway up their shins, letting the cold sink through to their bones. 'On this day, 1545, the Mary Rose sank. Seven hundred souls were lost,' said Jill, reading from the mid-section of a newspaper she'd brought to swat midges. 'Henry the eighth watched her capsize.'

'So...?' said Ailsa.

'So nothing. I'm just reading it out. Mark likes you.'

'Good for him.' The thought of being paired with a boy in her year made Ailsa feel like one of the pinned dragonflies in the nature cabinet. Jill had a boyfriend who went to a boarding school miles away. She claimed they were soulmates, but it seemed that there was not enough there of either of them to make sense of using that term. Ailsa had already considered going out with the boy in the café, but she'd dismissed the idea. There was a lone ash tree on the hill behind her family's house, it stood out twisting against the sky, and she thought of herself like that, rooted in her own space.

'He really likes you, I think,' said Jill, skimming a stone.

Ailsa let the silence string out thinly, then said. 'There was a whole flock of caterpillars on the road a couple weeks ago.'

'So...?' Jill said.

'So they were like a plague. I tried to save them.'

'Why bother?'

'If I was a caterpillar, I'd want someone to save me.'

'But you're not a caterpillar.'

'Even so.'

Mrs Graham lived in a one-floor, dark wood house that was attached to the back of the café. It had the appearance of a small, dry chocolate cake. Ailsa made a point of not looking at the house or the café if she had to pass them during the week.

On her third Saturday there, she cut her hand trying to pick up an empty glass bottle that had toppled from her tray and smashed. A lot of blood eased out of the cut. She stood and watched it for a while, then made her way to the kitchen and sat down on a stool. Mrs Graham came in behind her.

'What are you doing?' she said. 'Get that broken glass cleaned up, please.'

'My hand...' Ailsa pulled back her sleeve. The ground tilted unexpectedly at the second sighting of the blood.

'Put it under the tap, then clear up the glass.'

Ailsa stood, and the earth tipped further, but she kept upright and held her hand beneath the cold water. The blood didn't stop, but Mrs Graham was watching her so she traipsed back out and knelt and gathered the glass pieces carefully with a paper towel using the hand that wasn't bleeding. She carried them to the bin then brought a damp cloth and dabbed up the small flecks of glass. Mrs Graham observed her. After it was done, Ailsa returned to the kitchen and sat down again on the stool. 'Are you not going to go back to work?' Mrs Graham said.

'It's still bleeding.'

Mrs Graham stepped towards her and took her hand and turned it over. 'You have made a mess, haven't you?' she said. Her touch was cool and papery. She reached up to a cupboard and threw a roll of grey bandages into Ailsa's lap. The action made Ailsa want to throw them back at her head, but instead she looked down and concentrated on wrapping the bandages round and round her palm. There was nothing to stick them with, so she held them in place with her thumb for the rest of the shift.

At the end of the day, the kitchen assistant left the café just ahead of her. As he was unchaining his bike, he looked round.

'I think she's a robot,' he said. He was wearing the T-shirt he'd had on the first week. It looked now more like a coloured image of a brain scan than an inkblot test.

She smiled. 'Yeah, probably.' He cycled away in the opposite direction, and she headed for the road by the loch.

. . .

One Sunday, at closing time, Mrs Graham stood in front of the exit and faced her three employees. She held up a china figurine of a girl dancing in a tartan skirt.

'I want to know who broke this,' she said. It had always been broken. Ailsa had noticed it not long after she started. One of the dancing girl's arms curved round to her hip and it seemed that the other should have been stretched to the sky, but it was missing. The three of them stood there watching Mrs Graham as if she was a cat balancing on its hind legs.

'It's been like that for ages,' Ewan said finally.

'Don't be smart. It's valuable, I would have noticed if it was broken.' The figurine looked like it had come from a car boot sale. The paint was too gaudy, and dirt was ingrained in the varnish.

'Is no one going to own up to it?' Mrs Graham tapped one dull red shoe on the floor. 'Well, I suppose you'll just have to go for now but it diminishes my trust in you, that's all.' Ailsa bit the inside of her cheek to keep herself from laughing.

When she left to go home, Ewan was tinkering with the brake pads on his bike. She stopped near him, to rifle through her bag.

'Do you think they turn her off at night?' he said.

'Who's they?'

'I don't know, the people who programmed her.'

'Yeah, I suppose they do. To save power.'

He laughed. They were almost exactly the same height. She wanted something more to say to him so that he didn't go right away. 'What do you think of reincarnation?'

He wrinkled his nose. It caused him to look squirrel-ish. 'It's possible, I guess. I don't know.'

'What would you like to come back as?'

'A human,' he said.

'Me too.'

He got on his bike, and she stepped out of his way. He was carrying a backpack with a textbook sticking out of it. He let the bike slide down the hill without pedalling and waved a sort of salute over his shoulder. Watching him go, she felt a ticking against the insides of her elbows.

The next weekend, she was aware of a growing claustrophobia whenever Mrs Graham was near. Sometimes they would be pressed together as they both attempted to pass through the hatch in the counter at the same time, and her eyes would join with Mrs Graham's for a moment, and she would have the same sensation she got when looking into the eyes of a nervous, unstable collie dog out on one of the farms. At the close of the day, she made the mistake of leaving the café first and had no reason to wait for Ewan, so she walked straight home by herself.

The following Sunday was the busiest day so far, and the air of the café became warm and gluey by the late hours of the afternoon. Smiling at the customers made Ailsa's jaw tight. Mrs Graham wore a black ribbon at her neck, arranged in a way that resembled a bow tie. Ailsa had noticed that her outfits, which had been plain at first, seemed to be growing more fanciful. Yesterday she had worn almond-sized, tassled, gold earrings.

Come five o'clock, when Mrs Graham was at the back of the café, shutting up the windows, Ailsa made sure that she and Ewan were setting out to leave at the same moment. As they walked out together, her eye fell on the old telephone table by the door and the broken dancer figurine still sitting there. Ewan's gaze followed hers, and as they passed by, he reached out and lifted the statue into his coat with one swooping movement. She could sense why he did it. It was to do with the statue's ridiculousness and pointlessness, sitting there looking ugly and broken on the table.

When he had unchained his bike, he said, 'Come down to the loch?' He motioned with his head.

'OK.'

He started cycling with one hand, the other holding the statue to his chest, and she followed him. They headed down the road and cut through the nearest opening in the trees, out of sight of the café. A pebble-scattered, heather-clotted track led down to the water.

It was one of those rare days where the surface was still, mirroring the mountains. 'Let's see if the bitch can swim,' Ewan said quietly. Although he was referring to the china girl, she knew he was also talking about Mrs Graham. He took out the statue and hurled it forward. It broke the skin of the loch with a sound like a pike jumping. The rings stayed on the surface for a long time, zoning the disappearance point.

They stood side by side. A golden cloud of midges gathered over the water. It was usually quiet here, but now the lack of noise seemed so intense it was almost artificial, like someone had turned it on with a switch. He faced her and for a moment she thought that they were going to stay like that, frozen, but then he leaned forward to kiss her, without quite catching her lips full on. She opened her mouth, and the tip of her tongue touched his, and his mouth seemed to taste the same as hers, and she pulled her head back, and so did he.

The following weekend was their second last at the café. After that, the school term began and they would stop working. When Ailsa arrived, the cook was not in the kitchen and Mrs

Graham was busy scraping a spatula about inside a frying pan, a star-spangled apron tied twice around her midriff. At their lunchtime, Ailsa slid into the seat across from Ewan. Mrs Graham headed out through the side door. They could still see her through the whorled glass.

'Why's she cooking? Is Mateusz ill?'

'She fired him,' he said. 'For stealing.'

'Stealing what?' She leant forward on her elbows.

'Stealing the statue.'

'Shit, really? But why did she think it was him?' Dabs of coldness started over her back.

'She says she saw him. She's off her head.'

'She can't just sack him. He could sue her or something.'

'Well, I don't know, but he's not here today.'

The door swung open and Mrs Graham came in carrying a full bin bag. They sat back simultaneously and picked up their cutlery.

At the end of the day, Mrs Graham kept Ailsa behind for twenty minutes, scrubbing at some black marks on the carpet that wouldn't come out. Ailsa could not imagine what they were, and there was no moving them. Eventually, Mrs Graham sighed and let her go. When she stepped outside into the clean air, Ewan was there waiting for her, one arm looped around a tree.

They walked down to the loch, Ewan wheeling his bike beside her. It was raining, and the surface of the water seemed to rise up in points to meet the drops.

'I saw her throwing stones at a cat,' he said.

'Next week's the last week, thank fuck,' she said. She watched Ewan carefully out of the corner of her eye. 'You could still come through to the village, though, on your bike.'

'Yeah, I could.' He picked up a pebble and tossed it into the water without trying to skim it. 'We should do something, just before we go. Get her back a bit.'

'What sort of thing?'

'Put slug pellets in the food?'

'What if someone died?'

'You can't die from slug pellets. I don't think. It doesn't have to be that. What if we called a health inspector?'

'Is there anything that would get her in trouble?'

'We could make sure there was something,' he said.

'Like what?'

'I don't know, a road kill.' They both snorted.

'Let's do that,' she said.

'OK. I'll find something.'

He reached his hand to hers and she took it. His skin was cold. She looked down. He was wearing a black and orange bracelet with braided threads. She brushed it with her middle finger. 'It looks like some caterpillars I saw.'

'Yeah, I know. I saw them too. That's why I got it. They were all over the road.'

'It was the day I started.'

'They come every year,' he said. 'But I've never seen so many on the road.'

'It looked like someone had scattered them from the air.'

He turned to her, and they started kissing. She put her arms around his neck as she thought she should, but it seemed to set her off balance. She had a sense of switching, wanting to be both near and away. Drawing in his breath instead of air. Eventually, it was her that pushed him back, lightly by the shoulders, and she began heading off up the track.

. . .

On Friday, the day before the last weekend she would work at the café, she saw the Polish cook walking with his wife and their three black dogs on the loch shore. How did they ever tell the dogs apart? Even the three collars were a matching red. She had heard that Mateusz and his wife might move away, that they were fed up with the area. She could not see his expression and left the shore before he was close enough for her to be obliged to say something.

On the last day, the café was fairly busy again. Mrs Graham told Ailsa off for her unkempt hair, although she had always had it pretty much like that. Mrs Graham herself was wearing her hair up in an intricate kind of knot, as she'd never had it before, clipped with a brass butterfly.

Stepping into the kitchen with an order for omelettes, Ailsa whispered to Ewan, 'Have you brought something?'

He nodded.

'Show me.'

'Can't, it's taped up in a plastic bag. It would stink the place up.'

'What is it?'

'A dead rat. There's a farm by my house. They leave poison out.'

'What if she catches you?'

'I'll go back into the kitchen after she's checked it at the end of the day, say I've forgotten something.' Ailsa nodded, but she couldn't get any feeling about it, whether it was right or wrong.

The end of the day was slow coming. For a while, she had contemplated having her own outburst where she would tell Mrs Graham what she thought of her. But it didn't happen, and she had no appetite for it. 'Your pay will be through on

Friday,' was all Mrs Graham said of a goodbye. Her hair had come undone a little.

Ailsa got out and waited for Ewan by his bike.

He joined her, grinning. 'Sayonara,' he said to the café.

'Did it?'

'Done.'

The plan was for Ewan to ring the tourist board on Monday morning. Walking down the tree-shadowed tarmac, it seemed to Ailsa like a childish scheme, impossible that it could work. But there was a lightness in her limbs. Never to have to set foot in the café again.

It was a bright evening. The scents of the heather and the peat and the bog myrtle mixed warmly together. The two of them ambled down to the shore, and he struggled to pull something out of his backpack.

'What's that?' she asked.

'A blanket.'

They placed it on the moss-cushioned turf between the trees just before the stones of the water's edge. Bees hummed in the heather behind them. They sat and talked for a while and then lay down on their backs and folded the old tartan blanket over themselves and listened to the sound of the water.

He rolled on his side and then on top of her. They wriggled and fumbled, undoing their clothes. They had sex wrapped in the blanket. His breath came as if it was hard to catch. She guessed it was his first time. It was hers, and it hurt. She walked back in the dark with burrs in her hair and mud on her jeans and told her mother she had gone to Jill's house and fallen on the way home.

. . .

As the first weeks of term frittered by, she listened out for news about the café, but nothing came, and she waited for the sight of Ewan on his bike, but he did not appear. The café kept its handwritten, rectangular *Open* sign in the window, turned to the outside world.

.   .   .

They made their way to the village in a rented car. Ewan drove and Ailsa dozed in the passenger seat, sun flickering over her eyelids. When they reached the road along the loch shore, they found the café with its windows open, but the square wooden house was boarded up. They parked the car. The café seemed to have become a kind of makeshift art gallery; small, square canvases in the window. Ailsa asked inside about Mrs Graham, but the woman working there had never heard of her. 'We rent it from a French couple,' she said.

Ailsa walked by herself a little way. She reached the post office shop and wandered inside. It was all laid out the same, geraniums along the window, jumbled plastic toys for sale on the lower shelves, but behind the counter was someone she recognised. The Polish cook. He had stayed. He didn't seem to know her; she must look different. She could not immediately remember his name though she recalled the three black dogs he'd had, walking like a trio of shadows along the pebble shore. She asked about the café, not saying who she was, and he told her that Mrs Graham had drowned. 'About three or four years back now. She was in a small fishing boat, out by herself at three in the morning. God knows why. Some people thought she did it on purpose, but they ruled it an accident. A real shame. You knew her?'

'Very briefly, yes.'

He didn't ask how, so she didn't say. She bought stamps and candy hearts and went on her way as there were other customers queuing behind her. She'd heard her school friend Jill still lived in the village, but she had no urge to seek her out.

All those years ago, after she and Ewan had returned to school, the café had appeared to carry on as normal. No forced closure by health authorities. She didn't see Ewan until the winter break when they got together again at a dance in her village hall, the place peppered with white fairy lights. It had occurred to her by then that Ewan might not have done anything with the rat, or even had one at all, but she made a pact with herself not to ask him. A year later, they set off to America together and then on to Canada, working various café and bar jobs, legally and illegally. Ewan left her one night without saying anything and was gone for two months. The next thing she heard, he'd been involved in a car crash in which the driver died; he was the passenger. He had pink scars on his knees like roman numerals, which she traced with her fingers. Back together, they moved to Ireland, shared a flat for a while.

Now they'd travelled all the way here, and she was pregnant and plagued by morning sickness. They had returned to Scotland with a plan to tell her parents about the pregnancy. Her mum and dad had moved down to a house in Perthshire. She and Ewan had already visited them. They'd sipped cups of strong tea and balanced plates of Battenberg cake on their laps, and said none of what they had meant to say. Almost as if by not speaking, they were creating some leeway, keeping the glimmer of growing life unreal. She'd felt cocooned, sitting there in the new living room with the old furniture, the menagerie of china creatures on the mantelpiece. A day later, with nothing revealed, she and Ewan had set off on an unplanned trip north, saying it would be *interesting* to see the old places again.

Now, as she left the post office, she had a sense that they were in fact doing something unconstructive, allowing in a stale taste.

She returned to the car, and they drove towards the spot on the shore where they used to meet. She told Ewan about Mrs Graham. 'That's a shame,' he said as if he hadn't listened.

The curves in the road were sharp, the water appearing in flashes. Just before they reached the loch, she called for him to stop. Because moving across the tarmac were the bodies of fat, black and orange caterpillars. Not as many as she remembered, but a good number of them nonetheless. He braked.

'Look. Remember? Remember that happened before?' she said. She opened her door and undid her seatbelt. She badly wanted it to be a sign, but for what? He restarted the engine.

'Don't,' she said. 'There's caterpillars everywhere.'

'Damnit, we have to get on,' he said. 'What are you going to do, pick them all off the road?' He waited, and she shut the door again, and he drove forward. She sat with her eyes closed.

They came to the place by the loch, and he said, 'Do you want to stop here or not?' and she nodded.

She got out, and he stayed put, and she cut down to the shore and sat on a rock. She watched two small, bottle green rowing boats on the far side, which she supposed were like the vessel Mrs Graham had taken out that night, whether intending to die or not. The water was choppy, broken up into ripples. She rolled her socks off and dipped her toes in the coolness. She found herself wishing she had a way to know what Mrs Graham had meant to do, whether it was death she'd wanted.

After a time, Ewan called her. She dried her feet with her socks and pulled on her shoes. Following the old pathway, she returned to the car. They drove onwards, her damp socks laid out on the dashboard. Through the window beside her, the unreflective surface of the loch gave nothing away.

Dog's Bone

I was a small child then and could hardly begin to understand what had happened. To me, it was the start of autumn, a time of wet gold leaves sticking to the bathroom skylight, green and black confectionary appearing in the village shop. My parents sheltered me from the television news and I did not use the internet unsupervised. Mr Webster, the shop's owner, bought in pumpkins, extra turnips, and large bags of peanuts like he did every year. The air had started to sweeten with the scent of woodsmoke. We began using our own fireplace again, and it came to be a focus of attention for me. I'd bring in twigs and leaves to throw into the flames, to watch them snap and spark. 'Don't put too many wet twigs on, pet, we'll get smoked out like bees,' my mum said.

At school, we were making a giant skeleton for Halloween. Papier-mâché bones glued onto a huge sheet of black card, placed into an outline the teacher had drawn. 'Do you really think that's appropriate now?' one of the mothers asked our teacher at going-home time. There was a muffled conversation as I left, the two of them looking down at the half-formed skeleton, their hands on their hips.

'Why did she say that?' I asked my dad in the evening.

'I don't know, Elspie, she must have had her reasons.'

Really, I think I understood and was just checking my impression with an adult.

We carried on with our project. I liked making the bones out of newspapers and paste, shaping them like the dog toys they sold in the pet section of the store. In the end, the skeleton had eighty-two bones. We were proud of it and surprised to learn a real skeleton had far more.

Sometimes my parents talked about the news at home; we couldn't edge round it entirely. 'It won't affect us here,' my dad said. 'It's happened very far away.'

I began to drink hot milk at night like I used to when I was a much younger child. I'd sit up and watch nature documentaries with my mum, squashing in so close I was almost on her lap as pygmy elephants trotted across the screen. Or I'd play cards with my dad, snap or a simple version of blackjack, leaving the table to drop a piece of kindling in the fire every now and again. We took to placing a lit candle between us while we played, silent gaps filled up with the ticking of the clock above us.

It wasn't long before people started to arrive from further south. First, both the hotels were filled, every place taken on the caravan site, then people began to park cars and vans in the fields, setting up tents and paying a fee to the landowner. 'It won't last forever,' my dad said. 'People are afraid they might get sick down south. Once all the fuss dies away, they'll go home. They'll have to go anyway when the cold sets in.' We had a lot of new children to play with. They didn't go to the school, there wasn't room, but in the late afternoons and early evenings, the mix of us would gather in the park like baby goats collecting round a hay bale. There were always adults watching from the sidelines, a row of them marked by the shadow of the churchyard wall.

One day, my mum and I were walking on the beach when we noticed that the sand up ahead of us appeared duller than usual. As we made our way further along, we realised half of the west bay was covered in dead sea creatures. They were mainly starfish, their bodies a pale grey or pink as cooked salmon. I crouched down to peer at their whorled limbs. Amongst them, there was an octopus with lightless, coin-sized eyes. I studied it closely then moved further in among the bodies. Once I'd got a few metres from my mother, I began to have a scrabbling sensation on my skin, as if the dead things were touching me. I started to take in small suctions of air, a kind of inverse scream. My mother took me by the hand and led me home. Later, I asked if the sea creatures had died because of the bomb, and she said she didn't know. It could be a coincidence.

A word I was to notice a lot. In school, a girl sobbed because some of her hair came out as she was brushing it. 'That's just a coincidence, hair falls out sometimes,' the teacher said. Her voice was honey soft though the girl kept crying. 'You've got a dog, Mhairi. You know how they shed big clumps of fur over the furniture? Well, humans lose a wee bit of hair now and again. It's so nice new hair has room to grow.' Mhairi nodded, pink-eyed.

One night, drinking my warm milk, I said to my mum, 'I used to have a sippy cup.' I remembered it, the blue top, how I'd chew on the spout with my teeth.

'When you were a baby.'

'Can I have one now?'

'I don't think so love, they're for wee ones.'

'I am a wee one.'

'Not so much anymore. You're taller than me when you stand on a kitchen chair. Those cups are for wee ones who aren't at school yet.'

I carried on sipping the creamy milk from my mug. She watched me closely. 'You could have cocoa in that if you want. Make it into a hot chocolate like you had in the café. I could put cream on top.'

'I just want milk,' I said.

Later, I announced I'd buy a sippy cup from the local store with my pocket money. 'That's up to you,' my mum said.

The shop was attached to the post office, and the next day when my mum was buying stamps, I searched the mugs and plates. They didn't have sippy cups in, so I bought a dog's rubber bone toy instead. It was for the future, when we would have a dog, as my parents promised we would if ever one of them could work from home.

'That was sensible,' my mum said after I showed her what I'd bought. The bone was pink; I reasoned it wouldn't matter if the dog was a boy since dogs were colour-blind. At that time, my dad's job was to make deliveries all across the district. My mum worked in the office attached to the doctor's surgery and knew everyone's secrets.

'Can we get a dog if the school closes down?' I asked her. 'I'd be at home to look after it then.'

'Who said the school is closing down?'

'Just people.' It was something I'd heard discussed many times now by parents, children, teachers.

'If the school closes down, you'll have to go to the office with me or out in the van with dad.'

'Not if your work closes down too,' I said. I took the bone home and put it in my wicker basket of special things under my bed. From the window, I could see a dithering skein of geese going by. Below, the fields were full of brightly coloured tents. A few were now dotted amongst the heather further out.

The next day at school, during writing practise, a boy called Ruairi began making a thin keening noise. He was seated behind me. When I looked round, I saw that he held one of his teeth in his palm. He rocked back in his chair, his hand out flat, displaying it.

'That's a baby tooth,' said one of the girls.

'It's not, it's not, that one fell out before and it growed back and it's fallen out again and it's not supposed to,' he said. His palm closed up. He wiped his nose on the knee of his jeans. The teacher rose and guided him out of the class. She came back without him.

We carried on with our writing. We were each to produce a story about a castle full of ghosts. I took a lot of care with that kind of thing, picturing the layout of the castle. Mine had three floors and many windows. At last, the bell rang for home-time.

'How was today?' my mum asked as we were walking back up the oak tree path. I leant my head against her, my feet still stepping forward. She always wore the same perfume from a diamond-shaped bottle, it was so much the scent of her that I was suspicious of anyone else who wore it, as if they had stolen some of her essence.

'We wrote about castles,' I said. 'Ruairi cried.'

'What happened?'

'He got taken to the headteacher's.' It was either that or the nurse's office, but the headteacher sounded more dramatic.

'Well, Ruairi does get upset sometimes, doesn't he?'

'Yeah, he does,' I said. 'Like that time we played snakes and ladders, and I won, and he tipped the board on the floor.'

'Don't let him make you upset,' she said.

'I won't.' I kicked a pile of leaves and they flew ahead of me in an amber rush.

That weekend, we heard Ruairi's family were moving further north. Up to one of the islands where his cousins lived. 'Should we move to the islands?' I asked my dad. He had started to grow a prickly grey beard for no reason he could explain, my mum said he looked like a billy goat.

'It won't make a blind bit of difference,' he said. Then, 'We're safe here as it is. They're making a song and dance.'

The skeleton was displayed in the gym hall with a row of three carved pumpkins. The pumpkins were never lit because we were only in school in daylight hours, but I imagined them lighting themselves at night and turning to grin at each other. The late autumn gales began around that time. I'd sit still and listen to them for long stretches. Some nights the people in tents had to pack up and sleep in their cars and vans. I watched them, warm behind my bedroom window, as they held their hats to their heads, struggled with vehicle doors caught by the wind.

Over the weeks, several other families left for the islands, or arranged to drive south to catch flights to distant countries. Some of the people in the tents moved further north, including a few new friends I'd hoped to keep. I heard my parents talking from time to time about where we would go if we left, coming back to the fact that we would not go, there was no need.

I bought more items for the dog in hope of the school closing permanently: a tartan collar, a packet of dried treats, a squeaky rubber pheasant.

'Are you going to be getting a pup, young lady?' Mr Webster asked at the till.

'Potentially,' I said. He laughed and I blushed. I kept all the things I bought in the basket with the pink bone. I resisted buying a coat for the dog because I didn't know what size it would be.

One night in my room after I was supposed to be asleep, I put the light back on and I picked up my favourite book, one about a dog, a cat and a tortoise who go to live on a tropical island. It was full of colourful, detailed illustrations. I opened the first page and held it under the lamp. The familiar, chunky typeface. I stared at it. There was something wrong. I scrunched my eyes then looked at the page again. I couldn't read. Though I could sound out each individual letter, I could not get the words to make sense. It wasn't that they swam in front of my eyes but the opposite: they stayed stuck and stationary on the page. I had been proud of learning to read. In this moment, it seemed to me that I had unlearned. I hurtled myself out of bed and shouted for my parents. My dad came rushing in.

'What is it?'

'I can't read.'

'Of course you can read.'

'I can't, I can't,' I held the book upside down, let it drop onto the floor.

'Shh, you know how to read.'

'I forgot.'

'People don't forget how to read, Elspie.' He picked the book up and handed it to me. 'It's not the type of thing you can forget.' I took it from him and peered at the words on the open page. The words peered back. Glued in their places without meaning.

'I can't read. It's the bomb. It's in my brain,' I said. I dropped the book again, arms rigid by my sides.

'Of course it's not. That isn't possible.'

'It's brain-damaged me,' I said.

My father shook his head. He put the book back on the shelf. 'I think it's getting a bit late. This is what happens when children stay up too long.'

Eventually, he persuaded me to climb back into bed. I closed my eyes. After the light was put out, fiery alphabets flickered against my eyelids, and the quilt became too hot.

The next day, I tried not to look at any books or printed words, quickly averting my gaze from any writing I came across. My parents didn't ask me about my lost ability, so I didn't mention it.

On Monday, when I was back at school, I found I could read my open spelling jotter as normal, scanning it before I even remembered about not being able to read. Everything in the classroom stayed plain and ordinary, except that the clock above the times-table chart seemed to tick far louder than usual, so I worked with my head turned away from it.

Over the next few weeks, the weather grew colder, we had the first scatterings of snow, and bought in a new set of Christmas lights. I collected more rubber bones for the dog. The shop sold dried rawhide chews too, but I didn't touch those because they looked like parts of dead things, which after all they were.

We stayed put; we did not want to leave home. As with previous years, I measured winter settling in by the falling of the last leaves from the oak tree that sheltered at the side of our house. Once they were all gone, I sat at the top of the stairs and overheard my parents wondering aloud whether they would ever grow back. Somewhere not so far away, I knew because I'd heard the adults speak of it, there were whole forests where the trees had stopped like broken clocks.

ACKNOWLEDGEMENTS

Thank you to my mum and dad, Jane McDonagh and Mike McDonagh, for their boundless love and support. Thank you to all my family and friends, especially Fiona McBryde, Catriona Twigg, Betsy Andrews, Mel Grenfell, Elizabeth Welsh, Sharon Boateng, Hollie Ruddick, Alison Martin and my brother Steven McDonagh. Thank you to fellow writers who have given support and encouragement, particularly Devika Ponnambalam, Emily Prince and Fiona Robertson. Thank you to my colleagues at Health All Round, and to all the members of our community writing group. A big thank you to David Borrowdale at Reflex Press for taking a chance on this book.

Finally, so much love and thanks to my wonderful husband, Ross Galloway, for all his kindness, encouragement and love – the next book is for you...

. . .

The author and publisher wish to thank the editors of the publications in which the following stories first appeared, online or in print:

'Pony' first appeared in *The Lobsters Run Free* (Bath Flash Fiction Volume Two), December 2017; 'Owlets' – *For Books' Sake*, November 2018; 'Chicks' – (Part 1 of 'Owlets') as 'Owlets', *New Writing Scotland 35: She Said He Said I Said*,

August 2017; 'Air Gun' – (Part 2 of 'Owlets'), *The Nottingham Review*, September 2017.

REFLEX PRESS

Reflex Press is an independent publisher based in Abingdon, Oxfordshire, committed to publishing bold and innovative books by emerging authors from across the UK and beyond.

Since our inception in 2018, we have published award-winning short story collections, flash fiction anthologies, and novella-length fiction.

www.reflex.press
@reflexfiction